The Fab

MAG

TALES

Edited by

Kathleen Lines

ff

faber and faber

LONDON · BOSTON

First published in 1985
by Faber and Faber Limited
3 Queen Square, London WC1N 3AU

Printed in Great Britain by
Whitstable Litho Ltd., Whitstable, Kent
All rights reserved

British Library Cataloguing in Publication Data

[Tales of magic and enchantment. *Selections.*]
The Faber book of magical tales.
1. Tales   2. Legends
I. Title   II. Lines, Kathleen   III. Howard, Alan, *1922-*
398.2   PZ8.1

ISBN 0-571-13648-6

For
W.J.C.
In happy memory

CONTENTS

Contents

ACKNOWLEDGEMENTS

We are grateful for permission to use the following material: "The Feather of Finist the Falcon" from *Russian Wonder Tales* by Post Wheeler, published by A. S. Barnes & Co. Inc.; "Beowulf and Grendel" from *Beowulf* by Rosemary Sutcliff, reproduced by permission of The Bodley Head Ltd.; "The Birth of Pryderi" reprinted from *Welsh Legends and Folk-tales* retold by Gwyn Jones (1955), by permission of Oxford University Press; "Finn and the Young Hero's Children" from *The Well at the World's End* by Norah and William Montgomerie, reproduced by permission of The Bodley Head Ltd.; "Gareth and Linette" reprinted from *Stories of King Arthur and his Knights* retold by Barbara Leonie Picard (1955), by permission of Oxford University Press; "How Cormac Mac Art got his Branch" from *Shamrock and Spear* by F. M. Pilkington, reproduced by permission of The Bodley Head Ltd.; "Joseph and His Brethren" from *Stories from Holy Writ* by Helen Waddell, published by Constable & Co. Ltd.

"The Apple of Contentment" comes from *Pepper and Salt* by Howard Pyle, published by Harper & Row; "Caporushes" from *English Fairy Tales* by F. A. Steel, published by Macmillan & Co. Ltd.; "Oisin's Mother" from *Gods and Fighting Men* by Lady Gregory, published by John Murray Ltd.

FOREWORD

The Faber Book of Magical Tales is a selection from my earlier anthology *Tales of Magic and Enchantment*. It offers a choice of stories from different national traditions – fairy tales and also legends – for children who, already knowing nursery stories and humorous animal folk tales, are finding imaginative stimulus in the longer romantic fairy tale.

Popular fairytale themes recur again and again, and the same basic plot can be found in the folklore of many different races. Children can happily accept and feel quite at home with fairy tales from another country. The same is true of stories about legendary heroes, for it is often difficult to tell where fairy land ends and the realm of heroic romance begins; situations, incidents and even particular magical properties can be almost exactly identical.

In the traditional fairy tale much is demanded of the heroes and heroines – who are generally, and might just as well always be, nameless, for they are stock characters who behave as is necessary to the unfolding of the story. But the qualities that are often required of them, endurance, moral and physical courage, constancy in love, and sometimes self-sacrifice, are also found in the bardic tales and in the hero tales of the mediaeval cycles. In these legends, however, the character and personality of the hero gives an extra dimension and depth of feeling not usual in fairy tales; and although often he is helped or hindered by magic, tossed this way and that by the whim of the gods or by fate, it is his own strength or weakness that influences the progress of events. And these heroes, while they are drawn larger than life, do seem more real, nearer to mortal man, than do fairytale characters, and no matter how tremendously they strive, the ending of their story, as in life, is not necessarily a happy one.

Fairy tales, once they have given that first ecstatic delight and exercised the imagination, if not followed by more robust fare can become relegated to the past as a nostalgic memory. Romance literature — a vigorously peopled world on its own — opens out into wider and wider reaches. It would seem only natural that children who have shared the arduous tasks undertaken by fairytale prince or princess, the despised younger brother or the ill-treated little sister, should go on to read about King Arthur and his knights, Beowulf and Grendel, the pitiful enchantment of Sadbh, the stories of the grand Old Testament patriarchs, and other tales of long-ago heroes.

I am sorry that some of the stories in the second half are so short. It is not easy to take from a connected sequence of inter-related tales one incident that makes a good story, but these rather slight extracts (and the others too, of course) should serve as an introduction to fuller collections of hero tales and romantic legends.

I hope the wonder inherent in these tales of magic and enchantment will catch and hold the imagination of children. I'm sure they will find, as Ernest Rhys says in his preface to *Fairy Gold* (Dent), that the fairytale-tellers and romancers "swapped" their good things, and that there is a close kinship between these two branches of story-telling.

K.M.L.

FAIRY TALES FROM
FAR AND NEAR

The Princess sat on the roof of her palace (page 61)

THE APPLE OF CONTENTMENT

There was a woman once, and she had three daughters. The first daughter squinted with both eyes, yet the woman loved her as she loved salt, for she herself squinted with both eyes. The second daughter had one shoulder higher than the other, and eyebrows as black as soot in the chimney, yet the woman loved her as well as she loved the other, for she herself had black eyebrows and one shoulder higher than the other. The youngest daughter was as pretty as a ripe apple, and had hair as fine as silk and the colour of pure gold, but the woman loved her not at all, for, as I have said, she herself was neither pretty, nor had she hair of the colour of pure gold.

The first sister and the second sister dressed in their Sunday clothes every day, and sat in the sun doing nothing just as though they had been born ladies, both of them.

As for Christine—that was the name of the youngest girl—as for Christine, she dressed in nothing but rags, and had to drive the geese to the hills in the morning and home again in the evening, so that they might feed on the young grass all day and grow fat.

The first sister and the second sister had white bread (and butter beside) and as much fresh milk as they could drink; but Christine had to eat cheese-parings and breadcrusts, and had hardly enough of them to keep Goodman Hunger from whispering in her ear.

This was how the churn clacked in that house!

Well, one morning Christine started off to the hills with her flock of geese, and in her hands she carried her knitting, at which she worked to save time. So she went along the dusty road until, by-and-by, she came to a place where a bridge crossed the brook, and what should she see there but a little red cap, with a silver bell at the point of it, hanging from the alder branch. It was such a nice, pretty little red cap that Christine thought that she would take it with her, for she had never seen the like of it in all of her life before.

So she put it in her pocket, and then off she went with her geese again. But she had hardly gone two-score of paces when she heard a voice calling her, "Christine! Christine!"

She looked, and who should she see but a queer little grey man, with a great head as big as a cabbage and little legs as thin as young radishes.

"What do you want?" said Christine, when the little man had come to where she was.

Oh, the little man only wanted his cap again, for without it he could not go back home into the hill—that was where he belonged.

But how did the cap come to be hanging from the bush? Yes, Christine would like to know that before she gave it back again.

Well, the little hill-man was fishing by the brook over yonder when a puff of wind blew his cap into the water, and he just hung it up to dry. That was all that there was about it; and now would Christine please give it to him?

Christine did not know about that; perhaps she would and perhaps she would not. It was a nice, pretty little cap; what would the little underground man give her for it? that was the question.

Oh, the little man would give her five thalers for it, and gladly.

No; five thalers was not enough for such a pretty little cap—see, there was a silver bell hanging to it too.

Well, the little man did not want to be hard at a bargain; he would give her a hundred thalers for it.

No; Christine did not care for money. What else would he give for this nice, dear little cap?

"See, Christine," said the little man, "I will give you this for the cap," and he showed her something in his hand that looked just like a bean, only it was as black as a lump of coal.

"Yes, good; but what is that?" said Christine.

"That," said the little man, "is a seed from the apple of contentment. Plant it, and from it will grow a tree, and from the tree an apple. Everybody in the world that sees the apple will long for it, but nobody in the world can pluck it but you. It will always be

16

meat and drink to you when you are hungry, and warm clothes to your back when you are cold. Moreover, as soon as you pluck it from the tree, another as good will grow in its place. *Now*, will you give me my hat?"

Oh yes; Christine would give the little man his cap for such a seed as that, and gladly enough. So the little man gave Christine the seed, and Christine gave the little man his cap again. He put the cap on his head, and—puff!—away he was gone, as suddenly as the light of a candle when you blow it out.

So Christine took the seed home with her, and planted it before the window of her room. The next morning when she looked out of the window she beheld a beautiful tree, and on the tree hung an apple that shone in the sun as though it were pure gold. Then she went to the tree and plucked the apple as easily as though it were a gooseberry, and as soon as she had plucked it another as good grew in its place. Being hungry she ate it, and thought that she had never eaten anything as good, for it tasted like pancake with honey and milk.

By-and-by the oldest sister came out of the house and looked around, but when she saw the beautiful tree with the golden apple hanging from it you can guess how she stared.

The Apple of Contentment

Presently she began to long and long for the apple as she had never longed for anything in her life. "I will just pluck it," said she, "and no one will be the wiser for it." But that was easier said than done. She reached and reached, but she might as well have reached for the moon; she climbed and climbed, but she might as well have climbed for the sun—for either one would have been as easy to get as that which she wanted. At last she had to give up trying for it, and her temper was none the sweeter for that, you may be sure.

After a while came the second sister, and when she saw the golden apple she wanted it just as much as the first had done. But to want and to get are very different things, as she soon found, for she was no more able to get it than the other had been.

Last of all came the mother, and she also strove to pluck the apple. But it was no use. She had no more luck of her trying than her daughters; for all that the three could do was to stand under the tree and look at the apple, and wish for it and wish for it.

They are not the only ones who have done the like, with the apple of contentment hanging just above them.

As for Christine, she had nothing to do but to pluck an apple whenever she wanted it. Was she hungry? there was the apple hanging in the tree for her. Was she thirsty? there was the apple. Cold? there was the apple. So you see, she was the happiest girl betwixt all the seven hills that stand at the ends of the earth; for nobody in the world can have more than contentment, and that was what the apple brought her.

One day a king came riding along the road, and all of his people with him. He looked up and saw the apple hanging in the tree, and a great desire came upon him to have a taste of it. So he called one of the servants to him, and told him to go and ask whether it could be bought for a potful of gold.

So the servant went to the house, and knocked on the door— rap! tap! tap!

"What do you want?" said the mother of the three sisters, coming to the door.

Oh! nothing much; only a king was out there in the road, and wanted to know if she would sell the apple yonder for a potful of gold.

Yes, the woman would do that. Just pay her the pot of gold and he might go and pluck it and welcome.

So the servant gave her the pot of gold, and then he tried to pluck the apple. First he reached for it, and then he climbed for it, and then he shook the limb.

But it was no use for him to try; he could no more get it—well —than *I* could if I had been in his place.

At last the servant had to go back to the King. The apple was there, he said, and the woman had sold it, but try and try as he would he could no more get it than he could get the little stars in the sky.

Then the King told the steward to go and get it for him; but the steward, though he was a tall man and a strong man, could no more pluck the apple than the servant.

So he had to go back to the King with an empty fist. No; he could not gather it either.

Then the King himself went. He knew that he could pluck it— of course he could! Well, he tried and tried; but nothing came of his trying and he had to ride away at last without having had so much as a smell of the apple.

After the King came home, he talked and dreamed and thought of nothing but the apple; for the more he could not get it, the more he wanted it—that is the way we are made in this world. At last he grew melancholy and sick for want of that which he could not get. Then he sent for one who was so wise that he had more in his head than ten men together. This wise man told him that the only one who could pluck the fruit of contentment for him was the one to whom the tree belonged. This was one of the daughters of the woman who had sold the apple to him for the pot of gold.

When the King heard this he was very glad; he had his horse saddled, and he and his court rode away, and so came at last to the cottage where Christine lived. There they found the mother and the elder sisters, for Christine was away on the hills with her geese.

The King took off his hat and made a fine bow.

The wise man at home had told him this and that; now to which one of her daughters did the apple-tree belong? so said the King.

The Apple of Contentment

"Oh, it is my oldest daughter who owns the tree," said the woman.

So, good! Then if the oldest daughter would pluck the apple for him he would take her home and marry her and make a queen of her. Only let her get it for him without delay.

Prut! that would never do. What! was the girl to climb the apple-tree before the King and all of the court? No! No! Let the King go home, and she would bring the apple to him, all in good time; that was what the woman said.

Well, the King would do that, only let her make haste, for he wanted it very much indeed.

As soon as the King had gone, the woman and her daughters sent for the goose-girl to the hills. Then they told her that the King wanted the apple yonder, and that she must pluck it for her sister to take to him; if she did not do as they said they would throw her into the well. So Christine had to pluck the fruit; and as soon as she had done so the oldest sister wrapped it up in a napkin and set off with it to the King's house, as pleased as pleased could be. Rap! tap! tap! she knocked at the door. Had she brought the apple for the King?

Oh yes; she had brought it. Here it was, all wrapped up in a fine napkin.

After that they did not let her stand outside the door till her toes were cold, I can tell you. As soon as she had come to the King she opened her napkin. Believe me or not as you please, all the same, I tell you that there was nothing in the napkin but a hard round stone. When the King saw only a stone he was so angry that he stamped like a rabbit and told them to put the girl out of the house. So they did, and she went home with a flea in her ear, I can tell you.

Then the King sent his steward to the house where Christine and her sisters lived.

He told the woman that he had come to find whether she had any other daughters.

Yes; the woman had another daughter, and, to tell the truth, it was she who owned the tree. Just let the steward go home again and the girl would fetch the apple in a little while.

As soon as the steward had gone, they sent to the hills for

21

Christine again. Look! she must pluck the apple for the second sister to take to the King; if she did not do that they would throw her into the well.

So Christine had to pluck it, and gave it to the second sister, who wrapped it up in a napkin and set off for the King's house. But she fared no better than the other, for, when she opened the napkin, there was nothing in it but a lump of mud. So they packed her home again with her apron to her eyes.

After a while the King's steward came to the house again. Had the woman no other daughter than these two?

Well, yes; there was one, but she was a poor ragged thing, of no account, and fit for nothing in the world but to tend the geese.

Where was she?

Oh, she was up on the hills now tending her flock.

But could the steward see her?

Yes, he might see her, but she was nothing but a poor simpleton.

That was all very good, but the steward would like to see her, for that was what the King had sent him there for.

So there was nothing to do but to send to the hills for Christine.

After a while she came, and the steward asked her if she could pluck the apple yonder for the King.

Yes; Christine could do that easily enough. So she reached and picked it as though it had been nothing but a gooseberry on the bush. Then the steward took off his hat and made her a low bow in spite of her ragged dress, for he saw that she was the one for whom they had been looking all this time.

So Christine slipped the golden apple into her pocket, and then she and the steward set off to the King's house together.

When they had come there everybody began to titter and laugh behind the palms of their hands to see what a poor ragged goose-girl the steward had brought home with him. But for that the steward cared not a rap.

"Have you brought the apple?" said the King, as soon as Christine had come before him.

Yes; here it was; and Christine thrust her hand into her pocket and brought it forth. Then the King took a great bite of it, and as soon as he had done so he looked at Christine and thought that he had never seen such a pretty girl. As for her rags, he minded them no more than one minds the spots on a cherry; that was because he had eaten of the apple of contentment.

And were they married? Of course they were! and a grand wedding it was, I can tell you. It is a pity that you were not there; but though you were not, Christine's mother and sisters were, and, what is more, they danced with the others, though I believe they would rather have danced upon pins and needles.

"Never mind," said they; "we still have the apple of contentment at home, though we cannot taste of it." But no; they had nothing of the kind. The next morning it stood before the young Queen Christine's window, just as it had at her old home, for it belonged to her and to no one else in all of the world. That was lucky for the King, for he needed a taste of it now and then as much as anybody else, and no one could pluck it for him but Christine.

CAPORUSHES

Once upon a time, a long, long while ago, when all the world was young and all sorts of strange things happened, there lived a very rich gentleman whose wife had died leaving him three lovely daughters. They were as the apple of his eye, and he loved them exceedingly.

Now one day he wanted to find out if they loved him in return, so he said to the eldest, "How much do you love me, my dear?"

And she answered as pat as may be, "As I love my life."

"Very good, my dear," said he, and gave her a kiss. Then he said to the second girl, "How much do you love me, my dear?"

And she answered as swift as thought, "Better than all the world beside."

"Good!" he replied, and patted her on the cheek. Then he turned to the youngest, who was also the prettiest.

"And how much do *you* love me, my dearest?"

23

Now the youngest daughter was not only pretty, she was clever. So she thought a moment, then she said slowly:

"I love you as fresh meat loves salt!"

Now when her father heard this he was very angry, because he really loved her more than the others.

"What!" he said. "If that is all you give me in return for all I've given you, out of my house you go." So there and then he turned her out of the home where she had been born and bred, and shut the door in her face.

Not knowing where to go, the girl wandered on, and wandered on, till she came to a big fen where the reeds grew ever so tall and the rushes swayed in the wind like a field of corn. There she sat down and plaited herself an overall of rushes and a cap to match, so as to hide her fine clothes, and her beautiful golden hair that was all set with milk-white pearls. For she was a wise girl, and thought that in such lonely country, mayhap, some robber might fall in with her and kill her to get her fine clothes and jewels.

It took a long time to plait the dress and cap, and while she plaited she sang a little song:

> *"Hide my hair, O cap o' rushes,*
> *Hide my heart, O robe o' rushes.*
> *Sure! my answer had no fault,*
> *I love him more than he loves salt."*

And the fen birds sat and listened and sang back to her:

> *"Cap o' rushes, shed no tear,*
> *Robe o' rushes, have no fear;*
> *With these words if fault he'd find,*
> *Sure your father must be blind."*

When her task was finished she put on her robe of rushes and it hid all her fine clothes, and she put on the cap and it hid all her beautiful hair, so that she looked quite a common country girl. But the fen birds flew away, singing as they flew:

> *"Cap o' rushes, we can see,*
> *Robe o' rushes! what you be,*
> *Fair and clean, and fine and tidy,*
> *So you'll be whate'er betide ye."*

By this time she was very, very hungry, so she wandered on, and she wandered on; but ne'er a cottage or a hamlet did she see, till just at sun-setting she came on a great house on the edge of the fen. It had a fine front door to it; but mindful of her dress of rushes she went round to the back. And there she saw a strapping fat scullion washing pots and pans with a very sulky face. So, being a clever girl, she guessed what the maid was wanting, and said:

"If I may have a night's lodging, I will scrub the pots and pans for you."

"Why! Here's luck," replied the scullery-maid, ever so pleased. "I was just wanting badly to go a-walking with my sweetheart. So if you will do my work you shall share my bed and have a bite of my supper. Only mind you scrub the pots clean or cook will be at me."

Now next morning the pots were scraped so clean that they looked like new, and the saucepans were polished like silver, and the cook said to the scullion, "Who cleaned these pots? Not you, I'll swear." So the maid had to up and out with the truth. Then the cook would have turned away the old maid and put on the new, but the latter would not hear of it.

"The maid was so kind to me and gave me a night's lodging," she said. "So now I will stay without wage and do the dirty work for her."

So Caporushes—for so they called her since she would give no other name—stayed on and cleaned the pots and scraped the saucepans.

Now it so happened that her master's son came of age, and to celebrate the occasion a ball was given to the neighbourhood, for the young man was a grand dancer, and loved nothing so well as a country measure. It was a very fine party, and after supper was served, the servants were allowed to go and watch the quality from the gallery of the ballroom.

But Caporushes refused to go, for she also was a grand dancer, and she was afraid that when she heard the fiddles starting a merry jig, she might start dancing. So she excused herself by saying she was too tired with scraping pots and washing pans; and when the others went off, she crept up to her bed.

But alas! and alack-a-day! The door had been left open, and as she lay in her bed she could hear the fiddlers fiddling away and the tramp of dancing feet.

Then she upped and off with her cap and robe of rushes, and there she was ever so fine and tidy. She was in the ballroom in a trice joining in the jig, and none was more beautiful or better dressed than she. While as for her dancing . . . !

Her master's son singled her out at once, and with the finest of bows engaged her as his partner for the rest of the night. So she danced away to her heart's content, while the whole room was agog, trying to find out who the beautiful young stranger could be. But she kept her own counsel and, making some excuse, slipped away before the ball finished; so when her fellow-servants came to bed, there she was in hers in her cap and robe of rushes, pretending to be fast asleep.

Next morning, however, the maids could talk of nothing but the beautiful stranger.

"You should ha' seen her," they said. "She was the loveliest young lady as ever you see, not a bit like the likes o' we. Her golden hair was all silvered wi' pearls, and her dress—law! You wouldn't believe how she was dressed. Young master never took his eyes off her."

And Caporushes only smiled and said, with a twinkle in her eye, "I should like to see her, but I don't think I ever shall."

"Oh yes, you will," they replied, "for young master has ordered another ball tonight in hopes she will come to dance again."

But that evening Caporushes refused once more to go to the gallery, saying she was too tired with cleaning pots and scraping saucepans. And once more when she heard the fiddlers fiddling she said to herself, "I must have one dance—just one with the young master: he dances so beautifully." For she felt certain he would dance with her.

And sure enough, when she had upped and offed with her cap and robe of rushes, there he was at the door waiting for her to come; for he had determined to dance with no one else.

So he took her by the hand, and they danced down the ball-room. It was a sight of all sights! Never were such dancers! So young, so handsome, so fine, so gay!

27

But once again Caporushes kept her own counsel and just slipped away on some excuse in time, so that when her fellow-servants came to their beds they found her in hers, pretending to be fast asleep; but her cheeks were all flushed and her breath came fast. So they said, "She is dreaming. We hope her dreams are happy."

But next morning they were full of what she had missed. Never was such a beautiful young gentleman as young master! Never was such a beautiful young lady! Never was such beautiful dancing! Everyone else had stopped theirs to look on.

And Caporushes, with a twinkle in her eyes, said, "I should like to see her; but I'm *sure* I never shall!"

"Oh yes!" they replied. "If you come tonight you're sure to see her; for young master has ordered another ball in hopes the beautiful stranger will come again; for it is easy to see he is madly in love with her."

Then Caporushes told herself she would not dance again, since it was not fit for a gay young master to be in love with his scullery-maid; but, alas! the moment she heard the fiddlers fiddling, she just upped and offed with her rushes, and there she was fine and tidy as ever! She didn't even have to brush her beautiful golden hair! And once again she was in the ballroom in a trice, dancing away with the young master, who never took his eyes off her, and implored her to tell him who she was. But she kept her own counsel and only told him that she never, never, never would come to dance any more, and that he must say good-bye. And he held her hand so fast that she had a job to get away, and lo and behold! his ring came off his finger, and as she ran up to her bed there it was in her hand! She had just time to put on her cap and robe of rushes, when her fellow-servants came trooping in and found her awake.

"It was the noise you made coming upstairs," she made excuse; but they said, "Not we! It is the whole place that is in an uproar searching for the beautiful stranger. Young master he tried to detain her; but she slipped from him like an eel. But he declares he will find her; for if he doesn't he will die of love for her."

Then Caporushes laughed. "Young men don't die of love," says she. "He will find someone else."

But he didn't. He spent his whole time looking for his beautiful dancer, but go where he might, and ask whom he would, he never heard anything about her. And day by day he grew thinner and thinner, and paler and paler, until at last he took to his bed.

And the housekeeper came to the cook and said, "Cook the nicest dinner you can cook, for young master eats nothing."

Then the cook prepared soups, and jellies, and creams, and roast chicken, and bread sauce; but the young man would none of them.

And Caporushes cleaned the pots and scraped the saucepans and said nothing.

Then the housekeeper came crying and said to the cook, "Prepare some gruel for young master. Mayhap he'd take that. If not, he will die for love of the beautiful dancer. If she could see him now she would have pity on him."

So the cook began to make the gruel, and Caporushes left scraping saucepans and watched her. "Let me stir it," she said, "while you fetch a cup from the pantry-room."

So Caporushes stirred the gruel, and what did she do but slips young master's ring into it before the cook came back!

Then the butler took the cup upstairs on a silver salver. But when the young master saw it he waved it away, till the butler with tears begged him just to taste it.

So the young master took a silver spoon and stirred the gruel; and he felt something hard at the bottom of the cup. And when he finished it up, lo! it was his own ring! Then he sat up in bed and said quite loud, "Send for the cook!"

And when she came he asked her who made the gruel.

"I did," she said, for she was half-pleased and half-frightened.

Then he looked at her all over and said, "No, you didn't! You're too stout! Tell me who made it and you shan't be harmed!"

Then the cook began to cry. "If you please, sir, I *did* make it; but Caporushes stirred it."

"And who is Caporushes?" asked the young man.

"If you please, sir, Caporushes is the scullion," whimpered the cook.

Then the young man sighed and fell back on his pillow. "Send Caporushes here," he said in a faint voice, for he really was very near dying.

And when Caporushes came he just looked at her cap and her robe of rushes and turned his face to the wall; but he asked her in a weak little voice, "From whom did you get that ring?"

Now when Caporushes saw the poor young man so weak and worn with love for her, her heart melted, and she replied softly: "From him that gave it me." And she offed with her cap and robe of rushes, and there she was as fine and tidy as ever with her beautiful golden hair all silvered over with pearls.

And the young man caught sight of her with the tail of his eye, and sat up in bed as strong as may be, and drew her to him and gave her a great big kiss.

So, of course, they were to be married in spite of her being only a scullery-maid, for she told no one who she was. Now every one far and near was asked to the wedding. Amongst the invited guests was Caporushes' father, who, from grief at losing his favourite daughter, had lost his sight, and was very dull and miserable. However, as a friend of the family, he had to come to the young master's wedding.

Now the marriage feast was to be the finest ever seen; but Caporushes went to her friend the cook and said:

"Dress every dish without one mite of salt."

"That'll be rare and nasty," replied the cook; but because she prided herself on having let Caporushes stir the gruel, so saving the young master's life, she did as she was asked, and dressed every dish for the wedding breakfast without one mite of salt.

Now when the company sat down to table their faces were full of smiles and content, for all the dishes looked so nice and tasty; but no sooner had the guests begun to eat than their faces fell; for nothing can be tasty without salt.

Then Caporushes' blind father, whom his daughter had seated next to her, burst out crying.

"What is the matter?" she asked.

Then the old man sobbed, "I had a daughter whom I loved dearly, dearly. And I asked her how much she loved me, and she replied, 'As fresh meat loves salt.' And I was angry with her and turned her out of house and home, for I thought she didn't love me at all. But now I see she loved me best of all."

And as he said the words his eyes were opened, and there beside him was his daughter, lovelier than ever.

And she gave him one hand, and her husband, the young master, the other, and laughed saying, "I love you both as fresh meat loves salt." And after that they were all happy for evermore.

THE FEATHER OF FINIST THE FALCON

Once, in olden times, there was a merchant whose wife had died, leaving him three daughters. The eldest two were plain of face and hard of heart and cared for nothing but finery, while the youngest was a good housekeeper, kind-hearted, and so beautiful that it could neither be told in a tale nor written down with a pen.

One day, when the merchant set out for the Fair, he called his three daughters and asked: "My dear daughters, what do ye most desire me to buy for you?" The eldest answered: "Bring me a piece of rich brocade for a gown." The second said: "Bring me a fine scarf for a shawl." But the youngest replied: "Little father, bring me only a scarlet flower to set in my window."

The two sisters laughed at her request. "Little fool," they said, "what dost thou want of a scarlet flower? Thou wouldst better ask for a new apron." But she paid no heed and when the merchant asked her again, she said: "Little father, buy for me only the scarlet blossom."

The merchant bade them good-bye and drove to the Fair, and whether in a short while or a long while, he came again to his house. He brought the rich brocade for the eldest daughter and the fine scarf for the second, but he quite forgot to bring the little scarlet flower. The eldest daughters were so rejoiced at their gifts that he felt sorry for his forgetfulness, and to comfort her, said to the youngest: "Never mind, I shall soon go again to the Fair, and shall bring thee a gift also." And she answered: "It is no matter, little father; another time thou wilt remember." And while her

31

sisters, cutting and sewing their fine stuffs, laughed at her, she was silent.

Time passed, and again the merchant made ready to go to the Fair, and calling his daughters, he asked: "Well, daughters, what shall I buy for you?" The eldest answered, "Bring me a gold chain," and the second, "Buy me a pair of golden ear-rings," but the third said, "Little father, I want nothing but a scarlet flower to set in my window."

The merchant went to the Fair and he bought for the eldest daughter the chain and for the second the ear-rings, but again he forgot the scarlet flower. When he returned and the eldest two daughters took joy in their golden jewellery, he comforted the youngest as before, saying: "A simple flower is no great thing. Never mind. When I go again I shall bring thee a gift." And again she answered: "It is no matter, little father; another time perhaps I shall be luckier."

A third time the merchant made ready to go to the Fair, and called his three daughters and asked them what they most desired. The first answered, "Bring me a pair of satin shoes," the second said, "Buy me a silken petticoat," but the youngest said as before, "Little father, all my desire is for the scarlet flower to set in my window."

The merchant set out to the Fair, and he purchased the pair of satin shoes and the silken petticoat, and then he bethought himself of the scarlet flower and went all about inquiring for one. But search as he might, he could not find a single blossom of that colour in the whole town, and drove home sorrowful that he must disappoint his youngest daughter for the third time.

And as he rode along wondering where he might find the flower, he met by the roadside in the forest a little old man whom he had never seen, with a hooked nose, one eye, and a face covered with a golden beard like moss, who carried on his back a box.

"What dost thou carry, old man?" he asked.

"In my box," answered the old man, "is a little scarlet flower which I am keeping for a present to the maiden who is to marry my son, Finist the Falcon."

"I do not know thy son, old man," said the merchant, "nor yet the maiden whom he is to marry. But a scarlet blossom is no great thing. Come, sell it to me, and with the money thou mayest buy a more suitable gift for the bridal."

"Nay," replied the little old man. "It has no price, for wherever it goeth there goeth the love of my son, and I have sworn it shall be his wife's."

The merchant argued and persuaded, for now that he had found the flower he was loath to go home without it, and ended by offering in exchange for it both the satin shoes and the silken petticoat, till at length the little old man said: "Thou canst have the scarlet flower for thy daughter only on condition that she weds my son, Finist the Falcon."

The merchant thought a moment. Not to bring the flower would grieve his daughter, yet as the price of it he must promise to wed her to a stranger.

"Well, old man," he said, "give me the flower, and if my daughter will take thy son, he shall have her."

"Have no fear," said the little old man. "Whom my son woos, her will he wed!" and giving the box to the other, he instantly vanished.

The merchant, greatly disturbed at his sudden disappearance, hurried home, where his three daughters came out to greet him. He gave to the eldest the satin shoes and to the second the silken petticoat, and to see them they clapped their hands for delight. Then he gave to his youngest daughter the little box and said: "Here is thy scarlet flower, my daughter, but as for me, I take no joy of it, for I had it of a stranger, though it was not for sale, and in return for it I have promised that thou shalt wed his son, Finist the Falcon."

"Sorrow not, little father," said she. "Thou hast done my desire, and if Finist the Falcon will woo me then will I wed him." And she took out the scarlet flower and caressed it, and held it close to her heart.

When night came the merchant kissed his daughters, made over them the sign of the cross and sent them each to her bed. The youngest locked herself in her room in the attic, took the little flower from its box, and setting it on the window-sill, began to smell it and kiss it and look into the dark blue sky, when suddenly in through the window came flying a swift, beautiful falcon with

coloured feathers. It lit upon the floor and immediately was transformed into a young Prince, so handsome that it could not be told in speech nor written in a tale.

The Prince soothed her fright and caressed her with sweet and tender words so that she began to love him with such a joyful heart that one knows not how to tell it. They talked — who can tell of what? — and the whole night passed as swiftly as an hour in the daytime. When the day began to break, Finist the Falcon said to her: "Each evening when thou dost set the scarlet flower in the window I will come flying to thee. Tonight, ere I fly away as a falcon, take one feather from my wing. If thou hast need of anything, go to the steps under the porch and wave it on thy right side, and whatsoever things thy soul desireth, they shall be thine. And when thou hast no longer need of them, wave the feather on thy left side." Then he kissed her and bade her farewell, and turned into a falcon with coloured feathers. She plucked a single bright feather from his wing and the bird flew out of the window and was gone.

The next day was Sunday and the elder sisters began to dress in their finery to go to church. "What wilt thou wear, little fool?" they said to the other. "But for thy scarlet flower thou mightest have had a new gown, instead of disgracing us by thy appearance."

"Never mind," she said; "I can pray also here at home." And after they were gone she sat down at her attic window watching the finely-dressed people going to Mass. When the street was empty, she went to the steps under the porch and waved the bright feather to the right side, and instantly appeared a crystal carriage with high-bred horses harnessed to it, coachmen and footmen in gold livery, and a gown embroidered in all kinds of precious stones. She dressed herself in a moment, sat down in the carriage, and away it went, swift as the wind, to the church.

When she entered, so beautiful she was that all the people turned to look at her. "Some high-born Princess has come!" they whispered to each other; and in her splendid gown and head-dress even her two sisters did not recognize her as the one they had left in her little attic room. As soon as the choir began to sing the Magnificat she left the church, entered the crystal carriage and drove off so swiftly that when the people flocked out to stare there was no trace of her to be seen. As soon as she reached home she took off the splendid gown and put on her own, went to the porch, waved the bright feather to the left side and the carriage and horses, the coachmen in livery and the splendid gown disappeared, and she sat down again at her attic window.

When the elder sisters returned, they said: "What a beauty came today to church! No one could gaze enough at her. Thou, little slattern, shouldst have seen her rich gown! Surely she must have been a Princess from some other Province!"

Now so hastily had she changed her clothes that she had forgotten to take out of her hair a diamond pin, and as they talked her sisters caught sight of it. "What a lovely jewel!" they cried enviously. "Where didst thou get it?" And they would have taken it from her. But she ran to her attic room and hid it in the heart of the scarlet flower, so that though they searched everywhere they could not find it. Then, filled with envy, they went to their father and said: "Sir, our sister hath a secret lover who has given her a diamond ornament, and we doubt not that she will bring shame upon us." But he would not hear them and bade them look to themselves.

That evening when all went to bed, the girl set the flower on the window-sill, and in a moment Finist the Falcon came flying in and was transformed into the handsome Prince, and they caressed one another and talked together till the dawn began to break.

Now the elder sisters were filled with malice and spite and they listened at the attic door hoping to find where she had hidden the diamond pin, and so heard the voices. They knocked at the door crying: "With whom dost thou converse, little sister?"

"It is I talking to myself," she answered.

"If that is true, unlock thy door," they said.

Then Finist the Falcon kissed her and bade her farewell, and turning into a falcon, flew out of the window and she unlocked the door.

Her sisters entered and looked all about the room, but there was no one to be seen. They went, however, to their father and said: "Sir, our sister hath a shameless lover who comes at night into her room. Only just now we listened and heard them conversing." He paid no need, however, but chided them and bade them better their own manners.

Each night thereafter the spiteful pair stole from their beds to creep to the attic and listen at the door, and each time they heard the sound of the loving talk between their sister and Finist the Falcon. Yet each morning they saw that no stranger was in the room, and at length, certain that whoever entered must do so by the window, they made a cunning plan. One evening they pre-prepared a sweet drink of wine and in it they put a sleeping powder and prevailed on their sister to drink it. As soon as she did so she fell into a deep sleep, and when they had laid her on her bed, they fastened open knives and sharp needles upright on her window-sill and bolted the window.

When the dark fell, Finist the Falcon came flying to his love, and the needles pierced his breast and the knives cut his brilliant wings, and although he struggled and beat against it, the window remained closed. "My beautiful dearest," he cried, "hast thou ceased so soon to love me? Never shalt thou see me again unless thou searchest through three times nine countries, to the thirtieth Tzardom, and thou shalt first wear through three pair of iron shoes, and break in pieces three iron staves, and gnaw away three holy church-loaves of stone. Only then shalt thou find thy lover, Finist the Falcon!" But though through her sleep she heard these bitter words, still she could not awaken, and at last the wounded Falcon, hearing no reply, shot up angrily into the dark sky and flew away.

In the morning, when she awoke, she saw how the window had been barred with knives set cross-wise, and with needles, and how great drops of crimson blood were falling from them, and she began to wring her hands and to weep salt tears. "Surely," she thought, "my cruel sisters have made my dear love perish!" When she had wept a long time she thought of the bright feather, and ran to the porch and waved it to the right, crying: "Come to me, my own Finist the Falcon!" But he did not appear and she knew that the charm was broken.

Then she remembered the words she had heard through her sleep, and telling no one, she went to a smithy and bade the smith make her three pair of iron shoes, and three iron staves, and with these and three church-loaves of stone, she set out across three times nine countries to the thirtieth Tzardom.

She walked and walked, whether for a short time or a long time the telling is easy but the journey is not soon done. She wandered for a day and a night, for a week, for two months and for three. She wore through one pair of the iron shoes, and broke to pieces one of the iron staves, and gnawed away one of the stone church-loaves, when, in the midst of a wood which grew always thicker

and darker, she came to a lawn. On the lawn was a little hut on whose doorstep sat a sour-faced old woman.

"Whither dost thou hold thy way, beautiful maiden?" asked the old woman.

"O grandmother," answered the girl, "I beg for thy kindness! Be my hostess and cover me from the dark night. I am searching for Finist the bright Falcon, who was my friend."

"Well," said the dame, "he is a relative of mine: but thou wilt have to cross many lands still to find him. Come in and rest for the night. The morning is wiser than the evening."

The old woman gave the girl to eat and drink, a portion of all

The Feather of Finist the Falcon

God had given her, and a bed to sleep on, and in the morning
when the dawn began to break, she awoke her. "Finist, who flies
as the falcon with coloured feathers," she said, "is now in the
fiftieth Tzardom of the eightieth land from here. He has recently
proposed marriage to a Tzar's daughter. Thou mayest, perhaps,
reach there in time for the wedding feast. Take thou this silver
spindle; when thou usest it, it will spin thee a thread of pure gold.
Thou mayest give it to his wife for a wedding gift. Go now with
God across three times nine lands to the house of my second cousin.
I am bad-tempered but she is worse than I. However, speak her
fair and she may direct thee further."

The girl thanked the old woman and, bidding her farewell, set
out again, though with a heavier heart, on her journey. She walked
and walked, whether for a short time or a long time, across green
steppe and barren wilderness, until at length, when a second pair
of iron shoes were worn through, a second staff broken to pieces
and a second stone church-loaf gnawed away, she came one evening, on the edge of a swamp, to a little hut on whose doorstep sat
a second old woman, sourer than the first.

"Whither goest thou, lovely girl?" asked the dame.

"O grandmother," she answered, "grant me thy kindness. Be
my hostess and protect me from the dark night. I seek my dear
friend, who is called Finist the Falcon, whom my cruel sisters
wounded and drove from me."

"He is a relative of mine," said the old woman, "but thou wilt
have to walk many versts further to find him. He is to marry a
Tzar's daughter and today is her last maiden feast. But enter and
rest. The morning is wiser than the evening."

The old woman put food and drink before her and gave her a
place to sleep. Early on the morrow she woke her. "Finist the
Falcon," she said, "lives in the fiftieth land from here. Take with
thee this golden hammer and these ten little diamond nails. When
thou usest them, the hammer will drive the nails of itself. If thou
choosest thou mayest give them to his wife for a wedding gift. Go
now with God to the house of my fourth cousin. I am crabbed
but she is more ill-tempered than I. However, greet her with
politeness and perhaps she will direct thee further. She lives across
three times nine lands, beside a deep river."

39

The girl took the golden hammer and the ten little diamond
nails, thanked the old woman and went on her way. She walked
a long way and she walked a short way, and at last, when the
third pair of iron shoes were worn through, and the third iron
staff broken to pieces, and the third stone church-loaf gnawed
away, she came, in a dark wood where the tops of the trees touched
the sky, to a deep river and on its bank stood a little hut, on whose
doorstep sat a third old woman, uglier and sourer than the other
two put together.

"Whither art thou bound, beautiful girl?" asked the dame.

"O grandmother," she answered, "grant me a kindness. Be my
hostess and shield me from the dark night! I go to find Finist the
Falcon, my dearest friend, whom my sisters pierced with cruel
needles and knife-blades, and drove away bleeding."

"He is a relative of mine," said the old woman, "and his home
is not very far from here. But come in and rest this night; the
morning is wiser than the evening."

So the girl entered and ate and drank what the old woman
gave her, and slept till daybreak, when the other woke her and
said: "Finist the Falcon with coloured feathers is now in the next
Tzardom from here, beside the blue sea-ocean, where he stays at
the Palace, for in three days he is to marry the Tzar's daughter.
Go now with God and take with thee this golden saucer and this
little diamond ball. Set the ball on the plate and it will roll of
itself. Mayhap thou wilt wish to give them as a wedding gift to
his bride."

She thanked the old woman and started again on her way, and
in the afternoon she came to the blue sea-ocean spreading wide
and free before her, and beside it she saw a Palace with high
towers of white stone whose golden tops were glowing like fire.
Near the Palace a black serving-wench was washing a piece of
cloth in the sea, whose waves it tinged with red, and the girl said:
"What is it thou dost cleanse?"

The servant answered: "It is a shirt of Finist the Falcon who in
three days will wed my mistress, but it is so stained with blood
that I can by no means make it clean." The girl thought, "It is
a garment my beloved wore after he was so cruelly wounded by
the knives in my window!" And taking it from the other's hands,

she began to weep over it, so that the tears washed away every stain and the shirt was as white as snow.

The black serving-woman took the shirt back to the Tzar's daughter, who asked her how she had so easily cleansed it, and the woman answered that a beautiful maiden, alone on the sea-sand, had wept over it till her tears had made it white. "This is, in truth, a remarkable thing," said the Tzar's daughter; "I would see this girl whose tears can wash away such stains." And summoning her maids and nurses and attendants, she went walking along the shore.

Presently she came where the merchant's daughter sat alone on the soft sand gazing sorrowfully out over the blue sea-ocean, and she accosted her and said: "What grief hast thou that thy tears can wash away blood?"

"I grieve," answered the girl, "because I so long to see the beautiful Finist the Falcon."

Then the Tzar's daughter, being very prideful, tossed her head, saying: "Is that all? Go to the Palace kitchen, and I will let thee serve there; perchance as payment thou mayest catch a glimpse of him as he dines."

So the merchant's daughter entered the Palace and was given a humble place among the servants, and when Finist the Falcon sat him down to dine, she put the food before him with her own hands. But he, moody and longing for his lost love, sat without raising his eyes and never so much as saw her or guessed her presence.

After dinner, sad and lonely, she went out to the sea-beach and, sitting down on the soft sand, took her little silver spindle and began to draw out a thread. And in the cool of the evening the Tzar's daughter, with her attendants, came walking there and, seeing that the thread that came from the spindle was of pure gold, said to her: "Maiden, wilt thou sell me that plaything?"

"If thou wilt buy it at my price," answered the girl.

"And what is thy price?" asked the Tzar's daughter.

"Let me sit through one night by the side of thy promised husband," said the girl.

Now the Tzar's daughter was cold and deceitful, and desired Finist the Falcon, not because she loved him, but because of his beauty and her own pride. "There can be no harm in that," she thought, "for I will put in his hair an enchanted pin, by reason of which he will not waken, and with the spindle I can cover myself and my little mother with gold." So she agreed, and that night when Finist the Falcon was asleep, she put in his hair the enchanted pin, brought the girl to his room, and said: "Give me now the spindle, and in return thou mayest sit here till daybreak and keep the flies from him."

All night the girl bent over the bed where the handsome youth lay sleeping, and wept bitter tears. "Awake and rise, Finist, my bright Falcon," she cried. "I have come at last to thee. I have left my little father and my cruel sisters and I have searched through three times nine lands and a hundred Tzardoms for thee, my beloved!" But Finist slept on and heard nothing, and so the whole long night passed away.

And with the dawn came the Tzar's daughter and sent the girl back to the kitchen and she took away the enchanted pin so that Finist the Falcon should awaken.

When he came from his chamber, the Tzar's daughter said to him: "Hast thou rested well, and art thou refreshed?"

He answered: "I slept, but it seemed to me that someone was beside me all night, weeping and lamenting and beseeching me to awaken, yet I could not arouse myself, and because of that my head is heavy."

And she said: "Thou wert but dreaming! No one has been beside thee!" So Finist the Falcon called for his horse and betook himself to the open steppe a-hunting.

As it happened before, so it befell that day also. Finist the Falcon had no eyes for the girl who waited on him at table, and in the evening, sad and sorrowful, she went out to the blue sea-ocean, and sitting down on the soft sand, took out the golden hammer and the ten diamond nails and began to play with them. A little later the Tzar's daughter, with her maids and attendants, came walking along the beach, and seeing how the hammer drove the nails by itself, coveted the plaything and desired to buy it.

"It shall be thine," said the girl, "if thou wilt pay me my price."

"And what is the price?" asked the Tzar's daughter.

The Feather of Finist the Falcon

"Let me watch a second night beside the bed of thy promised husband."

"So be it," said the Tzar's daughter; and that night, after Finist the Falcon had fallen asleep, she put into his hair the enchanted pin, so that he could not waken, and brought the girl to his room. "Give me, now, the golden hammer and the diamond nails," she said, "and thou mayest keep the flies from him till day-dawn."

So that night too the merchant's daughter leaned over her beloved through the long dark hours, weeping and crying to him: "Finist my love, my bright Falcon, awake and speak to me! I have come at last to thee! I have journeyed to the fiftieth Tzardom of the eightieth land, and have washed the blood from thy shirt with my tears!" But because of the enchanted pin Finist could not waken, and at daybreak the girl was sent back to her place in the kitchen.

When Finist came from his chamber, the Tzar's daughter said: "Hast thou slept soundly, and art thou refreshed?"

He replied: "I slept, but it seemed to me that one I loved well bent over me, shedding bitter tears and begging me to arise, yet I could not wake. And because of this my own heart is heavy."

And she said: "It was but a dream that today's hunting will make thee speedily forget. No one was near thee while thou didst sleep." So Finist the Falcon called for his horse and rode to the open steppe.

That day the merchant's daughter wept and was exceedingly sorrowful, for on the morrow Finist the Falcon was to be wed. "Never again shall I have the love of my bright falcon," she thought. "Never more, because of my cruel sisters, may I call him to me with the little scarlet flower in my window!" When evening came, however, she dried her tears, sat down for a third time on the soft sand by the blue sea-ocean, and taking out the golden plate, set the diamond ball upon it. That evening also the Tzar's daughter, with her serving-women, came walking on the beach, and as soon as she saw how the little diamond ball was rolling, rolling of itself, she coveted it and said: "Wilt thou sell these also for the same price thou didst ask for thy other playthings?"

"Thou shalt have them," answered the merchant's daughter,

"for the same price. Let me only sit through this third night by the side of thy promised husband."

"What a fool is this girl!" thought the Tzar's daughter. "Presently I shall have all her possessions and Finist the Falcon for my husband into the bargain!" So she assented gladly and when Finist the Falcon fell asleep that night, for the third time she put into his hair the enchanted pin and brought the girl into his room, bidding her give over the golden plate and the diamond ball, and keep the flies from him till daybreak.

Through that long night also the merchant's daughter bent over her loved one, weeping and crying: "Finist, my own dear, my bright falcon with coloured feathers, awake and know me! I have worn through the three pairs of iron shoes, I have broken to pieces the three iron staves, I have gnawed away the three stone church-loaves, all the while searching for thee, my love!" But by reason of the enchanted pin, although he heard through his sleep her crying and lamenting, and his heart grieved because of it, Finist the Falcon could not waken. So at length, when day-dawn was near, the girl said to herself: "Though he shall never be mine, yet in the past he loved me, and for that I shall kiss him once before I go away," and she put her arms about his head to kiss him. As she did so, her hand touched the pin in his hair and she drew it out, lest by chance it harm him. Thus the spell of its enchantment was broken, and one of her tears, falling on his face, woke him.

And instantly, as he awoke, he recognized her, and knew that it was her lamenting he had heard through his sleep. She related to him all that had occurred, how her sisters had plotted, how she had journeyed in search of him, and how she had bought of the Tzar's deceitful daughter the three nights by his side in exchange for the silver spindle, the golden hammer and nails, and the diamond ball that rolled of itself. Hearing, Finist the Falcon was angered against the Tzar's daughter whom he had so nearly wed, but the merchant's daughter he kissed on the mouth, and turning into the falcon, set her on his coloured wings and flew to his own Tzardom.

Then he summoned all his princes and nobles and his officers of all ranks and told them the story, asking: "Which of these two am I to wed? With which can I spend a long life so happily that

44

it will seem a short one: with her who would deceitfully sell my hours for playthings, or with her who sought me over three times nine lands? Do ye now discuss and decide."

And all cried with one voice: "Thou shouldst leave the seller of thy rest and wed her who did follow thee!"

And so did Finist, the bright falcon with coloured wings.

HOW IAN DIREACH GOT THE BLUE FALCON

Long ago a king and queen ruled over the Islands of the West, and they had one son, whom they loved dearly. The boy grew up to be tall and strong and handsome, and he could run and shoot, and swim and dive better than any lad of his own age in the country. Besides, he knew how to sail a boat, and sing songs to the harp, and during the winter evenings, when everyone was gathered round the huge hall fire shaping bows or weaving cloth, Ian Direach would tell them tales of the deeds of his fathers.

So the time slipped by till Ian was almost a man, as they reckoned men in those days, and then his mother the queen died. There was great mourning throughout all the isles, and the boy and his father mourned her bitterly also; but before the new year came the king had married another wife, and seemed to have forgotten his old one. Only Ian remembered.

On a morning when the leaves were yellow in the trees of the glen, Ian slung his bow over his shoulder, and filling his quiver with arrows, went on the hill in search of game. But not a bird was to be seen anywhere, till at length a blue falcon flew past him, and raising his bow he took aim at her. His eye was straight and his hand steady, but the falcon's flight was swift, and he only shot a feather from her wing. As the sun was now low over the sea he put the feather in his game bag, and set out homewards.

"Have you brought me much game today?" asked his stepmother as he entered the hall.

"Nought save this," he answered, handing her the feather of

the blue falcon, which she held by the tip and gazed at silently. Then she turned to Ian and said:

"I am setting it on you as crosses and as spells, and as the fall of the year! That you may always be cold, and wet and dirty, and that your shoes may ever have pools in them, till you bring me hither the blue falcon on which that feather grew."

"If it is spells you are laying, I can lay them too," answered Ian Direach, "and you shall stand with one foot on the great house and another on the castle, till I come back again, and your face shall be to the wind, from wheresoever it shall blow." Then he went away to seek the bird, as his stepmother bade him; and, looking homewards from the hill, he saw the queen standing with one foot on the great house, and the other on the castle, and her face turned towards whatever tempest should blow.

On he journeyed, over hills, and through rivers till he reached a wide plain, and never a glimpse did he catch of the falcon. Darker and darker it grew, and the small birds were seeking their nests, and at length Ian Direach could see no more, and he lay down under some bushes and sleep came to him. And in his dream a soft nose touched him, and a warm body curled up beside him, and a low voice whispered to him:

"Fortune is against you, Ian Direach; I have but the cheek and the hoof of a sheep to give you, and with these you must be content." With that Ian Direach awoke, and beheld Gille Mairtean the fox.

Between them they kindled a fire, and ate their supper. Then Gille Mairtean the fox bade Ian Direach lie down as before, and sleep till morning. And in the morning, when he awoke, Gille Mairtean said:

"The falcon that you seek is in the keeping of the fierce Giant of the Five Heads, and the Five Necks, and the Five Humps. I will show you the way to his house, and I counsel you to do his bidding, nimbly and cheerfully, and, above all, to treat his birds well, for in this manner he may give you his falcon to feed and care for. And when this happens, wait till the giant is out of his house; then throw a cloth over the falcon and bear her away with you. Only see that not one of her feathers touches anything within the house, or evil will befall you."

"I thank you for your counsel," said Ian Direach, "and I will be careful to follow it." Then he took the path to the giant's house.

"Who is there?" growled the giant, when Ian Direach knocked loudly on the door of his house.

"One who seeks work as a servant," answered Ian Direach.

"And what can you do?" asked the giant again.

"I can feed birds and tend pigs; I can feed and milk a cow, and also goats and sheep, if you have any of these," replied Ian Direach.

"Then enter, for I have great need of such a one," said the giant.

So Ian Direach entered, and tended so well and carefully all the birds and beasts, that the giant was better satisfied than ever he had been, and at length he thought that Ian might even be trusted to feed the falcon. And the heart of Ian was glad, and he tended the blue falcon till his feathers shone like the sky, and the giant was well pleased; and one day he said to him:

"For long my brothers on the other side of the mountain have besought me to visit them, but never could I go for fear of my falcon. Now I think I can leave her with you for one day, and before nightfall I shall be back again."

Scarcely was the giant out of sight next morning when Ian Direach seized the falcon, and throwing a cloth over her head hastened with her to the door. But the rays of the sun pierced through the thickness of the cloth, and as they passed the door-post she gave a spring, and the tip of one of her feathers touched the post, which gave a scream, and brought the giant back in three strides. Ian Direach trembled as he saw him; but the giant only said:

"If you wish for my falcon you must first bring me the White Sword of Light that is in the house of the Big Women of Dhiur-radh."

"And where do they live?" asked Ian. But the giant answered:

"Ah, that is for you to discover." And Ian dared say no more, and hastened down to the waste. There, as he hoped, he met his friend Gille Mairtean the fox, who bade him eat his supper and lie down to sleep. And when he had wakened next morning the fox said to him:

"Let us go down to the shore of the sea." And to the shore of the sea they went. And after they had reached the shore, and beheld the sea stretching before them, and the Isle of Dhiurradh in the midst of it, the soul of Ian sank, and he turned to Gille Mairtean and asked why he had brought him thither, for the giant, when he had sent him, had known full well that without a boat he could never find the Big Women.

"Do not be cast down," answered the fox, "it is quite easy! I will change myself into a boat, and you shall go on board me, and I will carry you over the sea to the Seven Big Women of Dhiurradh. Tell these huge witches that you are skilled in brightening silver and gold, and in the end they will take you as servant, and if you are careful to please them they will give you the White Sword of Light to make bright and shining. But when you seek to steal it, take heed that its sheath touches nothing inside the house, or ill will befall you."

So Ian Direach did all the things as the fox had told him, and the Seven Big Women of Dhiurradh took him for their servant, and for six weeks he worked so hard that his seven mistresses said to each other: "Never has a servant had the skill to make all bright and shining like this one. Let us give him the White Sword of Light to polish like the rest."

Then they brought forth the White Sword of Light from the iron closet where it hung, and bade him rub it till he could see his face in the shining blade; and he did so. But one day, when the Seven Big Women were out of the way, he bethought him that the moment had come for him to carry off the sword, and, replacing it in its sheath, he hoisted it on his shoulder. But just as he was passing through the door the tip of the sheath touched it, and the door gave a loud shriek. And the Big Women heard it, and came running back, and took the sword from him, and said: "If it is our sword you want, you must first bring us the bay mare of the King of the Green Isle."

Humbled and ashamed, Ian Direach left the house, and sat by the side of the sea, and soon Gille Mairtean the fox came to him.

"Plainly I see that you have taken no heed to my words, Ian

Direach," said the fox. "But eat first, and yet once more will I help you."

At these words the heart returned again to Ian Direach, and he gathered sticks and made a fire and ate with Gille Mairtean the fox, and slept on the sand. At dawn next morning Gille Mairtean said to Ian Direach:

"I will change myself into a ship, and will bear you across the seas to the Green Isle, where dwells the King. And you shall offer yourself to serve in his stable, and to tend his horses, till at length so well content is he, that he gives you the bay mare to wash and brush. But when you run away with her see that nought except the soles of her hoofs touch anything within the palace gates, or it will go ill with you."

After he had thus counselled Ian Direach, the fox changed himself into a ship, and set sail for the Green Isle. And the King of that country gave into Ian Direach's hands the care of his horses, and never before did their skins shine so brightly or was their pace so swift. And the King was well pleased, and at the end of a month he sent for Ian and said to him:

"You have given me faithful service, and now I will entrust you with the most precious thing that my kingdom holds." And when he had spoken, he led Ian Direach to the stable where stood the bay mare. And Ian rubbed her and fed her, and galloped with her all round the country, till he could leave one wind behind him and catch the other which was in front.

"I am going away to hunt," said the King one morning while he was watching Ian tend the bay mare in her stable. "The deer have come down from the hill, and it is time for me to give them chase." Then he went away; and when he was no longer in sight, Ian Direach led the bay mare out of the stable, and sprang on her back. But as they rode through the gate, which stood between the palace and the outer world, the mare swished her tail against the post, which shrieked loudly. In a moment the King came running up, and he seized the mare's bridle.

"If you want my bay mare, you must first bring me the daughter of the King of the Franks, whom I have long desired as my wife."

How Ian Direach got the Blue Falcon

With slow steps went Ian Direach down to the shore where Gille Mairtean the fox awaited him.

"Plainly I see that you have not done as I bid you, nor will you ever do it," said Gille Mairtean the fox, "but I will help you yet again. For a third time I will change myself into a ship, and we will sail to France."

And to France they sailed, and, as he was the ship, the "Gille Mairtean" sailed where he would, and ran himself into the cleft of a rock, high on to the land. Then he commanded Ian Direach to go up to the King's palace, saying that he had been wrecked, that his ship was made fast in a rock, and that none had been saved but himself only.

Ian Direach listened to the words of the fox, and he told a tale so pitiful, that the King and Queen, and the Princess their daughter, all came out to hear it. And when they had heard, nought would please them except to go down to the shore and visit the ship, which by now was floating, for the tide was up. Torn and battered was she, as if she had passed through many dangers, yet music of a wondrous sweetness poured forth from within.

"Bring hither a boat," cried the Princess, "that I may go and see for myself the harp that gives forth such music." And a boat was brought, and Ian Direach stepped in to row it to the side of the ship.

To the further side he rowed, so that none could see, and when he helped the Princess on board he gave a push to the boat, so that she could not get back to it again. And the music sounded always sweeter, though they could never see whence it came, and sought it from one part of the vessel to another. When at last they reached the deck and looked around them, nought of land could they see, or anything save the rushing waters.

The Princess stood silent, and her face grew grim. At last she said:

"An ill trick you have played me! What is this that you have done, and whither are we going?"

"It is a queen you will be," answered Ian Direach, "for the King of the Green Isle has sent me to capture you, and in return he will give me his bay mare, that I may take her to the Seven

Big Women of Dhiurradh, in exchange for the White Sword of
Light. This I must carry to the giant of the Five Heads and
Five Necks and Five Humps, and in place of it, he will bestow
on me the blue falcon, which I have promised my stepmother,
so that she may free me from the spell which she has laid on
me."

"I would rather be wife to you," answered the Princess.

By-and-by the ship sailed into a harbour on the coast of the
Green Isle, and cast anchor there. And Gille Mairtean the fox
bade Ian Direach tell the Princess that she must bide yet a while
in a cave amongst the rocks, for they had business on land, and
after a while they would return to her. Then they took a boat and
rowed up to some rocks, and as they touched the land Gille Mairtean changed himself into a fair woman, who laughed and said
to Ian Direach, "I will give the King a fine wife!"

Now the King had been hunting on the hill, and when he saw
a strange ship sailing towards the harbour, he guessed that it
might be Ian Direach, and left his hunting, and ran down the
hill to the stable. Hastily he led the bay mare from her stall, and
put the golden saddle on her back, and the silver bridle over her
head, and with the mare's bridle in his hand, he hurried to meet
the Princess.

"I have brought you the King of France's daughter," said Ian
Direach. And the King of the Green Isle looked at the maiden,
and was well pleased, not knowing that it was Gille Mairtean the
fox. And he bowed low, and besought her to do him the honour
to enter the palace; and Gille Mairtean, as he went in, turned to
look back at Ian Direach, and laughed.

In the great hall the King paused and pointed to an iron chest
which stood in the corner.

"In that chest is the crown that has waited for you for many
years," he said, "and at last you have come for it." And he
stooped to unlock the box.

In an instant Gille Mairtean the fox in his own shape had
sprung on the King's back, and knocked him unconscious. The
fox then galloped away to the sea-shore, where Ian Direach and
the Princess and the bay mare awaited him.

"I will become a ship," cried Gille Mairtean, "and you shall go on board me." And so he did, and Ian led the bay mare into the ship and the Princess went after them, and they set sail for Dhiurradh. The wind was behind them, and very soon they saw the rocks of Dhiurradh in front. Then spoke Gille Mairtean the fox:

"Let the bay mare and the king's daughter hide in these rocks, and I will change myself into the mare, and go with you to the house of the Seven Big Women."

Glee and satisfaction filled the hearts of the Big Women when they beheld the bay mare led up to their door by Ian Direach. And the youngest of them fetched the White Sword of Light, and gave it into the hands of Ian Direach, who took off the golden saddle and the silver bridle, and went down the hill with the sword to the place where the Princess and the real mare awaited him.

"Now we shall have the ride that we have longed for!" cried the Seven Big Women; and they saddled and bridled the bay mare, and the eldest one got upon the saddle. Then the second sister sat on the back of the first, and the third on the back of the second, and so on for the whole seven. And when the witches were all seated, the eldest struck her side with a whip and the mare bounded forward. Over the moors she flew, and round and round the mountains, and still the Big Women clung to her and snorted with pleasure. At last the mare leapt high in the air, and came down on top of Monadh the high hill, where the crag is. And she rested her fore feet on the crag, and threw up her hind legs, and the Seven Big Women fell over the crag, and were dead when they reached the bottom. And the mare laughed, and became a fox again and galloped away to the sea-shore, where Ian Direach, and the Princess and the real bay mare and the White Sword of Light were awaiting him.

"I will make myself into a ship," said Gille Mairtean the fox, "and will carry you and the Princess, and the bay mare and the White Sword of Light, back to the land." And when the shore was reached, Gille Mairtean the fox took back his own shape, and spoke to Ian Direach in this wise:

"Let the Princess and the White Sword of Light, and the bay mare, remain among the rocks, and I will change myself into the likeness of the White Sword of Light, and you shall bear me to the giant, and, in exchange, he will give you the blue falcon."

And Ian Direach did as the fox bade him, and set out for the giant's castle. From afar the giant beheld the blaze of the White Sword of Light, and his fierce heart rejoiced; and he took the blue falcon and put it in a basket, and gave it to Ian Direach, who bore it swiftly away to the place where the Princess, and the bay mare, and the real Sword of Light were awaiting him.

So well content was the giant to possess the sword he had coveted for many a year, that he began at once to whirl it through the air, and to cut and slash with it. For a little while Gille Mairtean let the giant play with him in this manner; then he turned in the giant's hand, and cut through the Five Necks, so that the Five Heads rolled on the ground. Afterwards he went back to Ian Direach and said to him:

"Saddle the mare with the golden saddle, and bridle her with the silver bridle, and sling the basket with the falcon over your shoulders, and hold the White Sword of Light with its blade flat against your nose. Then mount the bay mare, and let the Princess mount behind you, and ride thus to your father's palace. But see that the sword is ever against your nose, else when your stepmother beholds you, she will change you into a dry faggot. If, however, you do as I bid, she will become herself a bundle of sticks."

Ian Direach hearkened to the words of Gille Mairtean, and his stepmother fell as a bundle of sticks before him; and he set fire to that evil woman, and was free from her spells for ever. After that he married the Princess, who was the best wife in all the Islands of the West. Henceforth he was safe from harm, for had he not the bay mare who could leave one wind behind her and catch the other wind, and the blue falcon to bring him game to eat, and the White Sword of Light to pierce through his foes?

And Ian Direach knew that all this he owed to Gille Mairtean the fox, and he made a compact with him that he might choose any beast out of his herds, whenever hunger seized him, and that henceforth no arrow should be let fly at him or at any of his race. But Gille Mairtean the fox would take no reward for the help he had given to Ian Direach, only his friendship. Thus all things prospered with Ian Direach till he died.

HOW THE RAJA'S SON WON THE
PRINCESS LABAM

In a country there was a Raja who had an only son who every day went out to hunt. One day the Rani, his mother, said to him, "You can hunt wherever you like on these three sides; but you must never go to the fourth side." This she said because she knew if he went on the fourth side he would hear of the beautiful Princess Labam, and that then he would leave his father and mother and seek for the princess.

The young prince listened to his mother, and obeyed her for some time; but one day, when he was hunting on the three sides where he was allowed to go, he remembered what she had said to him about the fourth side, and he was determined to go and see why she had forbidden him to hunt on that side. When he got there, he found himself in a jungle, and nothing in the jungle but a quantity of parrots, who lived in it. The young Raja shot at some of them, and at once they all flew away up to the sky. All, that is, but one, and this was their king, who was called Hiraman parrot.

When Hiraman parrot found himself left alone, he called out to the other parrots, "Don't fly away and leave me alone when the Raja's son shoots. If you desert me like this, I will tell the Princess Labam."

Then the parrots all flew back to their king, chattering. The prince was greatly surprised, and said, "Why, these birds can talk!" Then he said to the parrots, "Who is the Princess Labam? Where does she live?" But the parrots would not tell him where she lived. "You can never get to the Princess Labam's country," was all they would say.

The prince grew very sad when they would not tell him anything more; and he threw his gun away, and went home. When he got home, he would not speak or eat, but lay on his bed for four or five days, and seemed very ill.

At last he told his father and mother that he wanted to go and

find the Princess Labam. "I must go," he said. "I must see what she is like. Tell me where her country is."

"We do not know where it is," answered his father and mother.

"Then I must go and look for it," said the prince.

"No, no," they said, "you must not leave us. You are our only son. Stay with us. You will never find the Princess Labam."

"I must try and find her," said the prince. "Perhaps Providence or Khuda will show me the way. If I live and I find her, I will come back to you; but perhaps I shall die, and then I shall never see you again. Still, I must go."

So they had to let him go, though they wept at parting with him. His father gave him fine clothes to wear and a fine horse. And he took his gun, and his bow and arrows and a great many other weapons, "For," he said, "I may want them." His father, too, gave him plenty of rupees.

Then he himself got his horse all ready for the journey, and he said good-bye to his father and mother; and his mother took her handkerchief and wrapped some sweetmeats in it, and gave it to her son. "My child," she said to him, "when you are hungry, eat some of these sweetmeats."

The prince then set out on his journey, and rode on and on till he came to a jungle in which was a tank under shady trees. He bathed himself and his horse in the tank, and then sat down beneath a tree. "Now," he said to himself, "I will eat some of the sweetmeats my mother gave me, and I will drink some water and then I will continue my journey." He opened his handkerchief, and took out a sweetmeat. He found an ant in it. He took out another. There was an ant in that one too. So he laid the two sweetmeats on the ground, and he took out another, and another, and another, until he had taken them all out; but in each he found an ant. "Never mind," he said, "I won't eat the sweetmeats; the ants shall have them." Then the Ant-king came and stood before him and said, "You have been good to us. If ever you are in trouble, think of me and we will come to you."

The Raja's son thanked him, mounted his horse and continued his journey. He rode on and on until he came to another jungle, and there he saw a tiger who was roaring loudly as if from pain.

"Why do you roar like that?" said the young Raja. "What is the matter with you?"

"I have had a thorn in my foot for twelve years," answered the tiger, "and it hurts me so; that is why I roar."

"Well," said the Raja's son, "I will take it out for you. But perhaps, as you are a tiger, when I have made you well, you will eat me?"

"Oh, no," said the tiger, "I won't eat you. Do make me well."

Then the prince took a little knife from his pocket, and cut the thorn out of the tiger's foot; but when he cut the tiger roared louder than ever—so loud that his wife heard him in the next jungle, and came bounding along to see what was the matter. The tiger heard her coming and hid the prince in the jungle so that she should not see him.

"What man hurt you that you roared so loud?" said the wife.

"No one hurt me," answered the husband, "but a Raja's son came and took the thorn out of my foot."

"Where is he? Show him to me," said his wife.

"If you promise not to kill him, I will call him," said the tiger.

"I will not kill him; only let me see him," answered his wife.

Then the tiger called the Raja's son, and when he came the tiger and his wife made him a great many salaams. Then they gave him a good dinner, and he stayed with them for three days.

Every day he dressed the tiger's foot, and the third day it was quite healed. Then he said good-bye to the tigers, and they said to him, "If ever you are in trouble, think of us, and we will come to you."

The Raja's son rode on and on till he came to a third jungle. Here he found four fakirs whose teacher and master had died, and had left four things—a bed, which carried whoever sat on it whithersoever he wished to go; a bag, that gave its owner whatever he wanted, jewels, food, or clothes; a stone bowl that gave its owner as much water as he wanted, no matter how far he might be from a tank; and a stick and rope to which its owner had only to say, if any one came to make war on him, "Stick, beat as many men and soldiers as are here," and the stick would beat them and the rope would tie them up.

How the Raja's Son won the Princess Labam

The four fakirs were quarrelling over these four things. One said, "I want this"; another said, "You cannot have it, for I want it"; and so on.

The Raja's son said to them, "Do not quarrel for these things. I will shoot four arrows in four different directions. Whichever of you gets to my first arrow, shall have the first thing—the bed. Whoever gets to the second arrow, shall have the second thing— the bag. He who gets to the third arrow, shall have the third thing—the bowl. And he who gets to the fourth arrow, shall have the last things—the stick and rope." To this they agreed, and the prince shot off his first arrow. Away raced the fakirs to get it. When they brought it back to him he shot off the second, and when they had found and brought it to him he shot off his third, and when they had brought him the third he shot off the fourth.

While they were away looking for the fourth arrow, the Raja's son let his horse loose in the jungle, and sat on the bed, taking the bowl, the stick and rope, and the bag with him. Then he said, "Bed, I wish to go to the Princess Labam's country." The little bed instantly rose up into the air and began to fly, and it flew and flew till it came to the Princess Labam's country, where it settled on the ground.

Then the prince went on till he came to a house where he saw an old woman.

"Who are you?" she said. "Where do you come from?"

"I come from a far country," he said. "Will you let me stay with you tonight?"

"No," she answered, "I cannot let you stay with me; for our king has ordered that men from other countries may not stay in his country. You cannot stay in my house."

But the prince pleaded: "Let me remain with you for this one night. You see it is evening, and if I go into the jungle, then the wild beasts will eat me."

"Well," said the old woman, "you may stay here for tonight; but tomorrow morning you must go away, for if the king hears you have passed the night in my house, he will have me seized and put into prison."

Then she took him into her house, and the Raja's son was very glad. The old woman began preparing dinner, but he stopped her. "Wait," he said, "I will give you food." He put his hand into the bag saying, "Bag, I want some dinner," and the bag gave him instantly a delicious dinner, served up on two gold plates. The old woman and the Raja's son dined together.

When they had finished eating, the old woman said, "Now I will fetch some water."

"Don't go," said the prince. "You shall have plenty of water directly." So he took his bowl and said to it, "Bowl, I want some water," and then it filled with water. When it was filled the prince cried out, "Stop, bowl," and the bowl stopped filling.

By this time, night had come, and the Raja's son said to the old woman, "Why don't you light a lamp?"

"There is no need," she said. "Our king has forbidden the people in his country to light any lamps, for, as soon as it is dark, his daughter, the Princess Labam, comes and sits on her roof, and she shines so that she lights up all the country and our houses, and we can see to do our work as if it were day."

When it was quite black night, the princess got up. She dressed herself in her rich clothes and jewels, and rolled up her hair, and across her head she put a band of diamonds and pearls. Then she shone like the moon, and her beauty made night day. She came out of her room, and sat on the roof of her palace. In the daytime she never came out of her house; she only came out at night. All the people in her father's country then went about their work and finished it.

The Raja's son watched the princess quietly, and was very happy. He said to himself, "How lovely she is."

At midnight, when everybody had gone to bed, the princess came down from her roof, and went to her room; and when she was in bed and asleep, the Raja's son got up softly, and sat on his bed. "Bed," he said, "I want to go up to the Princess Labam's room." So the little bed carried him to the room where she lay fast asleep.

The young Raja took his bag and said, "Bag, I want a great deal of betel-leaf," and at once it gave him quantities of betel-leaf. This he laid on the carpet near the princess, and then his little bed carried him back to the old woman's house.

Next morning the princess's servants found the betel-leaf, and began to eat it. "Where did you get all that betel-leaf?" asked the princess.

"We found it near your bed," answered the servants. Nobody knew the prince had come in the night and put it all there.

At daybreak the old woman came to the Raja's son. "Now it is morning," she said, "and you must go; for if the king finds out what I have done for you he will seize me."

"I am ill today," said the prince, "do let me stay till tomorrow morning."

"Very well," said the old woman. So he stayed, and they took their dinner out of the bag, and the bowl gave them water.

When night came the princess got up and sat on her roof, and at twelve o'clock, when everyone was in bed, she went to her room, and was soon fast asleep. Then the Raja's son sat on his bed, and it carried him to the princess. He took his bag and said, "Bag, I want a most lovely shawl." It gave him a splendid shawl, and he spread it over the princess as she lay asleep. Then he went back to the old woman's house and slept till morning.

In the morning, when the princess saw the shawl, she was delighted. "See, mother," she said, "Khuda must have given me this shawl, it is so beautiful." Her mother was very glad too.

"Yes, my child," she said, "Khuda must have given you this splendid shawl."

When it was morning, the old woman said to the Raja's son, "Now you must really go."

"Ah, no," he answered, "I am not well enough yet. Let me stay a few days longer. I will remain hidden in your house, so that no one shall see me." So the old woman let him stay.

When it was black night, the princess put on her lovely clothes and jewels, and sat on her roof. At midnight she went to her room and went to sleep. Then the Raja's son sat on his bed and flew to her. He said to his bag, "Bag, I want a very, very beautiful ring." The bag gave him a glorious ring. Then he took the Princess Labam's hand gently to put on the ring, and she started up very much frightened.

"Who are you?" she said to the prince. "Where do you come from? Why are you in my room?"

"Do not be afraid, princess," he said. "I am no thief. I am a great Raja's son. Hiraman parrot, who lives in the jungle where I went to hunt, told me your name, and then I left my father and mother, and came to find you."

"Well," said the princess, "as you are the son of such a great Raja, I will not have you killed, instead I will tell my father and mother that I wish to marry you."

The prince then returned to the old woman's house. When morning came the princess said to her mother: "The son of a great Raja has come to this country, and I wish to marry him." Her mother told this to the king.

"Good," said the king, "but if this Raja's son wishes to marry my daughter, he must first do whatever I bid him. If he fails, he shall die."

In the morning the Raja's son told the woman that he intended to marry the princess. "Oh," said the old woman, "go away from this country, and do not think of marrying her. A great many Rajas and Rajas' sons have come here to woo her, and her father has had them all killed. He says whoever wishes to marry his daughter must first do whatever he bids them. If he can, then he shall marry the princess; if he cannot, the king will have him killed. But no one can do the things the king commands; so all the Rajas and Rajas' sons who have tried have been put to death. You will be killed too, if you try. Do go away." But the prince would not listen to anything she said.

The king sent to the old woman's house for the prince, and his servants brought the Raja's son to the king's courthouse to the king. There the king gave him eighty pounds of mustard seed and told him to crush all the oil out of it that day and bring it next morning to him to the courthouse. "Whoever wishes to marry my daughter," he said to the prince, "must first do all I tell him. If he cannot, then I have him killed. So if you cannot crush all the oil out of this mustard seed, you will die."

The prince was sad when he heard this. "How can I crush the oil out of all this mustard seed in one day?" he said to himself, "and if I do not, the king will kill me." He took the mustard seed to the old woman's house and did not know what to do. At last he remembered the Ant-king, and the moment he did so, the Ant-king and his ants came to him. "Why are you so downcast?" said the Ant-king.

The prince showed him the mustard seed, and said to him, "How can I crush the oil out of all this mustard seed in one day? And if I do not take the oil to the king tomorrow morning, I must die."

"Be happy," said the Ant-king, "lie down and sleep; we will crush all the oil out for you during the day, and tomorrow morning you shall take it to the king." The Raja's son lay down and slept and the ants crushed out the oil for him. The prince was very glad when he saw the oil.

The next morning he took it to the courthouse to the king. But the king said, "You cannot marry my daughter yet. If you wish to do so you must first fight with my two demons and kill them." The king a long time ago had caught two demons, and then, as he did not know what to do with them, he had shut them up in a cage. He was afraid to let them loose for fear they would eat up all the people in his country; and he did not know how to kill them. So all the kings and king's sons who wanted to marry the Princess Labam had to fight with these demons. "For," said the king to himself, "perhaps the demons may be killed, and then I shall be rid of them."

When he heard of the demons the Raja's son was very sad. "What can I do?" he said to himself. "How can I fight with these two demons?" Then he thought of his tiger; and the tiger and his wife came to him and said, "Why are you so sad?" The Raja's son answered, "The king has ordered me to fight with his two demons and kill them. How can I do this?" "Do not be frightened," said the tiger. "Be happy, I and my wife will fight them for you."

Then the Raja's son took out of his bag two splendid coats. They were all gold and silver and covered with pearls and diamonds. These he put on the tigers, and he took them to the king, and said to him, "May these tigers fight your demons for me?" "Yes," said the king, who did not care in the least who killed his demons, provided they were killed. "Then call your demons," said the Raja's son. The king did so, and the tigers and the demons fought and fought until the tigers had killed the demons.

"That is good," said the king. "But you must do something else before I give you my daughter. Up in the sky I have a kettle-drum. You must go and beat it. If you cannot do this, I will kill you."

The Raja's son thought of his little bed; so he went to the old woman's house and sat on his bed. "Little bed," he said, "up in the sky is a king's kettle-drum. I want to go to it." The bed flew up with him, and the Raja's son beat the drum and the king heard him. Still, when he came down, the king would not give him his daughter. "You have," he said to the prince, "done the three things I told you to do, but you must do one thing more." "If I can, I will," said the Raja's son.

Then the king showed him the trunk of a tree that was lying near his courthouse. It was a huge and very thick tree-trunk. He gave the prince a wax hatchet, and said, "Tomorrow morning you must cut this trunk in two with this wax hatchet."

The Raja's son went back to the old woman's house. He was very sad, and thought that now the Raja would certainly kill him. "I had his oil crushed out by the ants," he said to himself. "I had the demons killed by the tigers. My bed helped me to beat his kettle-drum. But now what can I do? How can I cut that thick tree-trunk in two with a wax hatchet?"

That night he went on his bed to see the princess. And he said to her, "Tomorrow your father will kill me."

"Why?" asked the princess.

"He has told me to cut a thick tree-trunk in two with a wax hatchet. How can I ever do that?" said the Raja's son. "Do not be afraid," said the princess, "do as I bid you, and you will cut it quite easily."

Then she pulled out a hair from her head and gave it to the prince. "Tomorrow," she said, "when no one is near you, you must say to the tree-trunk, 'The Princess Labam commands you to let yourself be cut in two by this hair.' Then stretch the hair down the edge of the wax hatchet's blade."

The prince, next day, did exactly as the princess had told him; and the minute the hair that was stretched down the edge of the hatchet-blade touched the tree-trunk it split into two pieces.

The king said, "Now you can marry my daughter." Then the wedding took place. All the Rajas and kings of the countries round were asked to come to it, and the feasting lasted many days. Then after a short while the Raja's son said to his wife, "Let us go to my father's country." The Princess Labam's father gave them a quantity of camels and horses and rupees and servants; and they travelled in great state to the prince's country, where they were welcomed, amid great rejoicing, by the prince's parents and all the people.

The prince always kept his bag, bowl, bed and stick; only as no one ever came to make war on him, he never needed to use the stick.

THE LAD WHO WENT TO THE NORTH WIND

Once upon a time there was an old widow who had one son; and one day, as she was feeling ill and weak, her son had to go out and up into the safe to fetch meal for cooking. But when he got outside the safe, and was just going down the steps, there came the North Wind puffing and blowing, caught up the meal, and so away with it through the air. Then the lad went back into the safe for more, but when he came out again on the steps, if the North Wind didn't come again and carry off the meal with a puff; and, more than that, he did so the third time. At this, the lad got very angry; and as he thought it hard that the North Wind should behave so, he thought he'd just look him up, and ask him to return the meal.

So off he went; but the way was long, and he walked and walked; but at last he came to the North Wind's house.

"Good day!" said the lad, "and thank you for coming to see us yesterday."

"GOOD DAY!" answered the North Wind, for his voice was loud and gruff, "AND THANKS FOR COMING TO SEE ME. WHAT DO YOU WANT?"

"Oh!" answered the lad, "I only wished to ask you to be so good as to let me have back that meal you took from me on the

safe steps, for we haven't much to live on; and if you're to go on snapping up the morsel we have, there'll be nothing for it but to starve."

"I haven't got your meal," said the North Wind, "but if you are in such need, I'll give you a cloth which will get you everything you want, if you only say, 'Cloth, spread yourself, and serve up all kinds of good dishes!'"

With this the lad was well content. But as the way was so long, he couldn't get home in one day, so he turned into an inn on the road; and when they were going to sit down to supper he laid the cloth on a table which stood in the corner, and said:

"Cloth, spread yourself, and serve up all kinds of good dishes!"

He had scarce said so before the cloth did as it was bid, and all who stood by thought it was a fine thing, but most of all the landlord. So, when all were fast asleep at dead of night he took the lad's cloth and put another in its stead, just like the one he had got from the North Wind, but which couldn't so much as serve up a bit of dry bread.

So, when the lad woke he took his cloth and went off with it, and that day he got home to his mother.

"Now," said he, "I've been to the North Wind's house and a good fellow is he, for he gave me this cloth, and when I only say to it, 'Cloth, spread yourself, and serve up all kinds of good dishes,' I get any sort of food I please."

"All very true, I dare say," said his mother, "but seeing is believing, and I shan't believe it till I see it."

So the lad made haste, drew out a table, laid the cloth on it and said:

"Cloth, spread yourself, and serve up all kinds of good dishes."

But never a bit of dry bread did the cloth serve up.

"Well," said the lad, "there's no help for it but to go to the North Wind again." And away he went.

So he came to where the North Wind lived late in the afternoon.

"Good evening," said the lad.

"Good evening," said the North Wind.

"I want my rights for that meal of ours which you took," said the lad. "As for that cloth I got, it isn't worth a penny."

The Lad who went to the North Wind

"I've got no meal," said the North Wind, "but yonder you have a ram which coins nothing but golden ducats as soon as you say to it, 'Ram, ram, make money!'"

So the lad thought this a fine thing; but as it was too far to get home that day, he turned in for the night to the same inn where he had slept before.

Before he called for anything, he tried the truth of what the North Wind had said of the ram, and found it all right; but, when the landlord saw that, he thought it was a famous ram, and, when the lad had fallen asleep, he took another which couldn't coin gold ducats, and changed the two.

Next morning off went the lad, and when he got home to his mother, he said:

"After all, the North Wind is a jolly fellow; for now he has given me a ram which can coin golden ducats if only I say, 'Ram, ram, make money!'"

"All very true, I dare say," said his mother, "but I shan't believe any such stuff until I see the ducats made."

"Ram, ram, make money!" said the lad; but if the ram made anything, it wasn't money.

So the lad went back again to the North Wind, and blew him up, and said the ram was worth nothing, and that he must have his rights for the meal.

"Well!" said the North Wind, "I've nothing else to give you but that old stick in the corner yonder; but it's a stick of a particular kind. If you say, 'Stick, stick, lay on!' it lays on till you say, 'Stick, stick, stop now!'"

So, as the way was long, the lad turned in this night too to the landlord; but as he could pretty well guess how things stood as to the cloth and the ram, he lay down at once on the bench and began to snore as if he were asleep.

Now the landlord, who easily saw that the stick must be worth something, hunted up one which was like it, and, when he heard the lad snore, was going to change the two; but, just as the landlord was about to take his stick, the lad bawled out:

"Stick, stick, lay on!"

So the stick began to beat the landlord, till he jumped over the chairs and tables and benches, and yelled and roared:

69

"Oh my, oh my! bid the stick be still, else it will beat me to death, and you shall have back your cloth and your ram."

When the lad thought the landlord had got enough, he said: "Stick, stick, stop now."

Then he took the cloth and put it into his pocket, and went home with his stick in his hand, leading the ram by a cord round its horns. And so he got his rights for the meal he had lost.

LITTLE FOOL IVAN AND THE LITTLE HUMPBACK HORSE

In Russia in days of old there once lived a peasant who had three sons—Vanya, Peter and Little Fool Ivan. Vanya and Peter were smart young fellows, and cunning in buying and selling; no one ever cheated them out of a bargain. But the youngest, Ivan, was quite different. After work, when his brothers would drive into town to feast and dance and have a gay time of it, he preferred to stay at home and play on his guitar, or to sit and sleep by the stove. So he became known as Little Fool Ivan, and his father and brothers thought him of no account.

Little Fool Ivan and the Little Humpback Horse

Now, in this year, crops had been poor and roubles were scarce. The peasant hoped for a good harvest. Daily he watched the grain in the great field as it ripened. Great was his dismay, therefore, when one morning he saw that a long strip had been cut from the almost ripe wheat.

"Some miserable thief is at work," he cried. And he told Vanya to sit up that night and watch.

It was a cold night and the wind blew up clouds to cover the moon. Vanya shivered and quickly became tired of the discomfort, so he rolled himself in his warm cloak and, finding a sheltered spot in the hedge, was soon fast asleep. When he awoke in the morning he saw that more corn had been cut. He roughed up his clothes and returned home.

"Have you caught the thief?" asked his father.

"I heard him in the dark," answered Vanya. "I shouted and tried to catch him, but because I could not see I fell and bruised myself badly. But I frightened him off, you may be sure of that."

The father praised his brave son, and said that Peter should watch that night. That second night was much like the first except that the rain poured down.

"What thief will come on a night like this and why should I become soaked to the skin?" said Peter to himself. He found a comfortable corner in a barn nearby and quickly fell asleep.

In the morning another strip of corn had been taken. He went to the brook and splashed water over himself and then returned home.

"Did you catch the thief?" asked his father.

"Yes, indeed I did," answered Peter. "We had a fierce struggle, but just as I thought I had him he slipped from my grasp and ran away. He is too frightened to come again, you may be sure of that. But what a night I have had! I am wet through."

The father praised his son, but wondered what should be done next.

"We must prepare to cut the grain, even though it is not yet ready," he said, "or we will lose it all."

"Father, I will watch tonight," said Little Fool Ivan.

"Much good will that do," said the father. "How can you hope to succeed where your brothers have failed?" But he allowed

71

himself to be persuaded, so when night fell Little Fool Ivan took
his guitar and went out into the field. He did not look for a place
to sleep as his brothers had done, instead first he walked round the
whole field, and then found a good perch in the forked branch of
a tree and played soft tunes to pass the time.

Suddenly, when the moon was high in the sky and it must have
been about midnight, he heard the whinny of a horse. He looked
out between the leaves and there, at the far edge of the field,
cropping the wheat, was a beautiful white mare with a mane of
golden curls and a golden tail. Little Fool Ivan watched as she
came nearer and nearer, and then with a sudden jump he was on
her back, holding tightly to her mane. The mare tossed her head
and snorted, and reared, trying to shake him off. Then, as he still
clung tightly, she shot forward at great speed. She sped over the
fields, and raced with the wind into the mountains and against
the wind into the forests; she sprang high in the air, and furiously
stamped upon the ground. But race and rear as she would she
could not throw off Little Fool Ivan. He clung to her neck and
mane and all the time he whispered in her ear, "Stop, stop now,
and don't be frightened. After all, it is you who are at fault, you
have taken my father's grain, but, beautiful creature, I will not
harm you." Then, suddenly, just before dawn was breaking the
mare stood still. "Well, Ivan," she said, "you have conquered
me, and you have shown great courage. Let me go now and in
three nights I will come again with treasures which will more than
repay your father for the grain he has lost. This I promise if you
in return will promise to tell no one."

So Little Fool Ivan promised to keep silent, and to be in the field
again at midnight three nights from then. The beautiful mare instantly disappeared—vanishing, it seemed, into a shaft of moonlight.

When Little Fool Ivan returned home he was greeted with scorn
by his father and brothers. "Where is the thief?" they asked. "We
made sure a clever lad like you would have captured him!"

"I've had a night of it, I can tell you," replied Ivan. "I jumped
on the thief's back and have flown over mountains and through
forests for miles and miles. I'm tired out." And he curled himself
up by the stove and was soon asleep. But the others laughed in
derision, for not a word did they believe.

73

Little Fool Ivan and the Little Humpback Horse

On the third night Little Fool Ivan crept out to the field. He had not long to wait. The moon came from behind a cloud and suddenly standing before him was the beautiful white mare, her tail and mane gleaming in the soft light. Beside her stood three colts. Two were magnificent creatures with dappled coats, eyes blue like sapphires, golden manes and tails, and hoofs that shone like diamonds. The third was a strange little brown horse, only three foot high, with a hump on its back and ears nearly touching the ground.

Then the mare said, "These are the treasure I promised. Two are king's horses; they will bring riches to your family. The third is for you, and for you alone. Keep him always and he will always be your friend. In all things he will serve you faithfully, but never must you sell him or part with him to another." When she had spoken thus she vanished. Little Fool Ivan rubbed his eyes. Had he been dreaming? No, for there beside him were the three horses the magic white mare had brought him. The little humpback horse came confidently towards him and gently nuzzled his hand, while the other two stood quietly. Ivan led the three to a disused stable, where he made them comfortable, and then went home to his bed with a light heart. What a surprise he would have for his father and brothers in the morning! He would go early to the stable, brush and polish the beautiful dappled horses and lead them to his father. "Here, father, is what the thief has sent you in payment for the grain you have lost."

But that night Little Fool Ivan slept soundly. He did not hear his brothers getting up before daybreak. They had decided to take what beasts they could spare to the Horse Fair in the big city, and wished to be in good time. Needing an extra halter Peter went to the old stables to look for one, and what was his astonishment when he found the strange horses there. He ran to fetch Vanya.

"Where can these marvellous creatures have come from?" each said to the other. "Can it be that this is what Little Fool Ivan has had on his mind? Sure it is that he has behaved strangely these last few days." Then Vanya said, "Here is the end to all our poverty. These two horses are fit only for the Tzar. They will bring us many hundreds of roubles if we take them to the Fair. Let us tell no one but be off quickly. You and I can divide most of the money between us." Peter agreed, and at once the brothers rode off, leading the two beauties. They had hardly noticed the strange little humpback horse.

When Little Fool Ivan awoke it was mid-morning. Hurriedly he went out to the stable. Two stalls were empty, the beautiful horses had vanished! As he stood there, not knowing what to do, so shocked and filled with despair, the little humpback horse whinnied, then spoke in human voice.

"Don't worry, dear master. Your brothers have stolen the horses and gone to the Fair. But jump on my back and we will overtake them." Hardly believing, Little Fool Ivan sat astride the little horse, who shot off like an arrow. So fast was his speed that he seemed to fly through the air, his long ears flapping like streamers in the wind. Over the fields they went and along the highway to the city. When they reached the outskirts the little horse stopped.

"Here we will wait for your brothers," he said. And sure enough in no time at all Vanya and Peter rode up, leading the two beautiful stallions. When his brothers saw Little Fool Ivan and his strange little horse in front of them, they did not know what to do. When he reproached them for taking the horses they protested that they had meant no harm.

"Dear Brother," said Vanya, "we could not be sure that the horses were yours, but even so we did not take them to wrong you."

"You know little of the trade and the business of bargaining," said Peter. "Vanya and I will sell them at a far better price."

"And so," continued Vanya, "as this season has been a hard one, we knew that you would rejoice with us when we returned with bags full of money."

"Your words sound fair enough," said Little Fool Ivan. "We will all go to the Fair and you may sell the horses."

And so, although the brothers wished Little Fool Ivan miles away, they all proceeded to the Fair.

When they reached the market-place where all the traders were, the wonderful horses caused a great commotion. People pressed close in on all sides, and so great were the crowds around them that none could pass either in or out. Wondering what was the cause of the excitement, the head-horseman of the Tzar's stables,

accompanied by soldiers, rode amongst the crowd and dispersed them. When he saw the horses, he proclaimed that no one was to bid for them, and quickly he went to the palace to inform the Tzar of what he had seen. When the Tzar heard of the wonderful steeds he called immediately for his coach and drove to the market.

There were the beautiful dappled horses, their manes and tails shining golden in the light, and their eyes flashing sapphire blue. They tossed their heads and pawed the ground with their delicate feet. The Tzar marvelled; never had he possessed such handsome animals. He went up to them, patted and caressed them, and asked who owned them.

"O Lord Tzar," said Ivan, "the horses are mine, and these are my brothers who have come here to sell them for our old father, for we are poor."

When Vanya named two thousand roubles as the price, the Tzar smiled. "I shall buy them," he said, "but I have never seen such beautiful creatures. I shall give double what you ask."

So the Tzar's paymaster handed over a bag of gold and five caps full of silver; then ten royal grooms in scarlet uniforms led the two horses away.

But as Little Fool Ivan and his two brothers were starting on the way home the two wonderful horses came galloping back. They had bitten through their bridles and knocked down the grooms. The Tzar came after them furiously in his coach. "I have bought your horses," he said, "but it seems I must have you too." And the little humpback horse whispered in Ivan's ear, "They will behave only for you." So Ivan agreed, on the condition that his little humpback horse should go too. He took leave of his brothers, and enjoined them to care for their father for the rest of his days with the gold and silver they were taking home.

Then the Tzar proclaimed Little Fool Ivan to be master of his stables, and Ivan led the two horses to the royal stables, closely followed by his little humpback horse, while the wondering crowds looked on.

Weeks passed. Ivan wore robes of scarlet and black, he ate well whenever he hungered and slept his fill. He took out the horses every morning at sunrise to gallop over the dewy fields, and groomed them till their coats shone like satin. He kept their stalls clean and bright, polished their bridles and harness, and cared for them in every way. There was no happier lad in all the land than Little Fool Ivan, and in all he did the little humpback horse was his friend and companion.

The Tzar was pleased with his new servant, but there were those at the court who were envious. And none more so than the man who had been Master of the Tzar's Horse before Ivan's arrival. This Stefan thought and thought on how he might bring about his rival's ruin. Often he hid in the stables watching to see if he could catch Ivan out in some fault. When this failed, and when he realized that many of the courtiers were also jealous of Ivan's success, he conspired with them. "Go about with downcast eyes and sorrowful expression," he said, "and when the Tzar asks the reason, I will tell such a tale that Ivan's fall from favour will be certain."

So when the Tzar asked his boyars why they looked so worried and sorrowful, Stefan spoke up. "O Mighty Tzar, it is not for themselves that they grieve, but for your royal person. All your loyal servants fear that the new Master of the Stables is evil and experienced in black magic. For we have heard him boast that he could, if he would, obtain for your Tzar's majesty the fabled sow with the golden bristles, together with her twenty piglets, who lives in a hidden valley in the Land of the South."

Hearing this the Tzar's eyes blazed with anger. "Bring me this boaster," he commanded. "He shall prove his words or forfeit his life."

So when Little Fool Ivan was brought before him the Tzar said, "You have boasted that you can fetch the sow with the golden bristles from the Land of the South. Listen then to my command; bring me this sow together with her twenty piglets, within the space of three days. If you fail you will lose your life."

Little Fool Ivan went out to the stables weeping bitterly. He could not imagine the reason for the Tzar's anger, and he knew nothing of the fabulous sow and her young. When the little humpback horse saw his master in tears, he asked, "Why are you not merry, little master? Why are you so sorrowful?"

Ivan lovingly embraced his little friend, and told him of the strange command the Tzar had laid upon him. "Don't distress yourself," said the horse. "What the Tzar desires is by no means impossible. But go first to him and ask for a bucket of golden corn, and a bucket of rosy apples, and a fine long cord of silk."

So Ivan went to the Tzar and asked for the corn and the apples and the silken cord, and brought them to the stable. "Now lie down and sleep," said the little humpback horse, "for wisdom comes with the morning." Little Fool Ivan lay down to sleep.

At dawn he was wakened by the little humpback horse. "It is time to go, for the way is long," said the little horse. "Take up the buckets of corn and apples and wind the cord round your waist, get on my back, and we will be off."

Off they went, swift as an eagle's flight, over fields and plains, across deep rivers and high up into the mountains. After travelling for a day and a night, the little horse brought Ivan into a deeply-wooded valley and there he stopped. "This is the secret valley, little master, which is the home of the sow with the golden bristles. Put the rosy apples and the golden corn on the ground at some distance from each other, and then hide in the thicket. Soon the sow will come to feed. She will make at once for the corn, while the piglets will snuff among the apples. Quickly take up the little ones and tie them with the silken lasso to my saddle, then get on my back, and we will set off on our return. The sow will follow where her young are taken."

Little Fool Ivan and the Little Humpback Horse

So Little Fool Ivan did as he was told, and hid behind a bush near to the pile of apples. Soon the sow came into sight, surrounded by her piglets. She began to eat the corn, while the piglets ran to the sweet-smelling apples. Ivan swiftly caught them up one by one and tied them with the silken cord to the saddle-bow. At this instant the sow saw what was happening and rushed upon them. But Ivan sprang astride the little horse and they were off. Away went the little horse at great speed back the way they had come, and the sow followed after.

In the space of a night and a day they came to the Tzar's palace after dark. Little Fool Ivan put the sow and her piglets into a pen; then he and the little humpback horse went to the stables and soon were fast asleep.

The Tzar was astonished next morning to find that Ivan had accomplished his task. In great delight with his new possessions he rewarded Ivan with gold and praised his courage. This made Stefan and the boyars still more envious of Ivan, and they plotted again to bring about his ruin.

So Stefan went to the Tzar. "Gracious Majesty," he said, "the Master of the Horse now boasts that what he has accomplished is nothing. He could, if he would, capture the mare with seven manes, and her seven fierce stallions from the great green field that lies in the high shining mountains."

The Tzar, whose heart was now filled with greed, sent for Little Fool Ivan.

"Listen to my command," he said. "Fetch me from the high mountains the seven-maned mare and her seven fierce stallions. If you have not accomplished this within the space of seven days, you will hang and the crows will pick your bones."

Sadly Ivan went to the little humpback horse and told him of the Tzar's desire. "Cheer up, little master," said the horse. "I can help you, and this task is not impossible. But go first to the Tzar, ask him to have built a marble stable with two doors, one opening in and one opening outwards. Ask him as well for the weightiest of iron clubs and the skin of a horse."

So Ivan asked for the stable, the iron club and the horse's skin. When all was ready the little horse said, "Dear master, lie down and sleep, wisdom comes with a new day."

Little Fool Ivan and the Little Humpback Horse

At dawn the little horse wakened his master. Ivan took up the iron club and the horse's skin, mounted the little horse, and away they flew.

When they had travelled for three days and three nights the little humpback horse stopped in a green plain between two high shining hills.

"This is where the seven-maned mare and her seven stallions graze every evening. Put the horse's skin over me and fasten it tightly. When the mare sees me she will at once set upon me. You must strike her between the eyes with the iron bar; this will stupefy her and you will be able to lead her away. As for the seven stallions, they will follow where the mare goes."

So Little Fool Ivan put the skin on the little humpback horse. When the wild horses came, the stallions grazed some way off but the mare saw the little horse at once and set upon him, and as she began to tear off the false skin Ivan ran up and struck her between the eyes and stunned her. Then quickly he got astride the little horse and, grasping the mare by the hair of her seven manes, led her off. The little horse went like the wind and the seven stallions galloped after—screaming with rage.

They travelled back the way they had come, and in the dark of the very last day they reached the Tzar's palace. The little humpback horse galloped straight into the marble stable. "Loose the mare," he whispered to Ivan, and then he ran out of the other door, which Ivan shut and barred. The mare and the seven stallions, which had followed closely, were thus held captive.

Then Little Fool Ivan and his friend the little horse went to their place and to sleep.

Next morning the Tzar was even more delighted than before. Never had any other Tzar possessed such treasures as these that Little Fool Ivan had brought him. So he bestowed still greater honours upon Ivan, till the envious boyars hardly knew how to contain their jealousy. Then they plotted again with Stefan, and one came to the Tzar and said: "O Mighty Tzar! Know that the Master of the Horse is boasting that what he has done is nothing. He could bring you, if he wished, the beautiful princess who lives in the land at the very edge of the world, where the red sun rises in flames behind the sea."

Little Fool Ivan and the Little Humpback Horse

Now the Tzar had long desired this princess for his wife, so he sent for Little Fool Ivan. "Bring me the princess who lives far from here in the land at the very edge of the world. If you succeed within twelve days I will give you much treasure. If you fail, your head will be struck from your shoulders."

Ivan wept bitter tears at this command. He knew nothing about the beautiful princess, and the task seemed impossible to perform.

But the little hunchback horse comforted him. "Dry your tears, master," he said. "This is a hard task but it is not impossible. But first, go to the Tzar and ask him for a silken tent, with gold and silver hangings, and an embroidered cloth, and a silver basket filled with choice foods and wine." And Ivan went to the Tzar, who gave him all he asked for.

Then said the little horse, "Lie down and sleep. Wisdom comes with the morning." And Ivan slept till the little horse wakened him at daybreak. Then, gathering up the silken tent and the silver basket, Ivan mounted the little horse, who sped on the way swift as lightning.

For five days they travelled over seven times seven countries, and then they reached the shore at the very edge of the world, where the sun rises fiery-red at the rim of the green-blue sea.

"Set up the tent upon the sand," said the little horse. "Inside spread out the embroidered cloth and upon it lay the food and wine. Then hide behind the tent and watch."

"Which way will the princess come?" asked Ivan, when he had set up the tent.

"It is her custom to sail upon the sea in a golden boat," answered the little horse. "From the water she will see the gleaming tent and will come ashore to look closer. Wait till she is inside, and is tempted by the delicacies you have set out there. Then swiftly enter and hold her fast. I will then come to your aid. But take care that you do nothing to alarm her."

The little horse ran off out of sight into the woods which touched the shore, and Ivan set himself behind the tent to wait.

Sure enough, before long there was the princess in her golden boat. As she dipped her silver oars in the calm water her eye was caught by the strange and lovely little tent upon the sand. Nearer and nearer she steered her boat, and then she rowed to the shore, grounded her boat upon the white sand, and came up to the tent and peeped inside.

Now Little Fool Ivan had made a small hole in the silk through which he could see. When the princess entered the tent he was overcome by her beauty. Her loveliness was beyond the power of tongue to tell or pen to describe. Forgetting the warning of the little horse, Ivan pressed his eye closely to the hole he had made, and in so doing he shook the silken side of the tent. The gold and silver hangings swayed, as if blown by a gentle wind. The princess took fright, ran back to her boat and quickly rowed away.

When the little humpback horse came running up Ivan was weeping for his stupidity.

"I forgot your warning," he said, "now I have frightened the princess away and I shall never see her again."

"Never mind," said the little horse, "the princess will come back tomorrow. But that will be your last chance. If you fail then we must go back to the Tzar without her, and your life will be forfeit."

Next day Little Fool Ivan spread out the wine and food, and hid behind the tent to watch. As before, the princess came in her golden boat. She walked up the sand and into the silken tent, and began to taste the food and drink the wine. And while she ate and drank Ivan caught her and held her fast, and called to the little humpback horse. The princess cried out in fright and struggled to be free. But when she had looked again at Little Fool Ivan she stopped struggling. Then Ivan held her before him on the saddle and the little horse flew like lightning back along the way they had come.

They travelled for six days and on the seventh they came again to the Tzar's city. With a sad and heavy heart (for he had fallen in love with her himself) Ivan led the lovely princess into the palace.

The Tzar was overjoyed. He set the princess beside him on a seat of purple velvet under a golden canopy, and addressed her in loving tones. "Welcome, O most lovely Princess. Long has my heart yearned for you, and I have had no rest, neither by day or night, thinking of your great beauty. You shall be my bride."

But the princess turned her eyes away and made no answer, though again and again he wooed her with fair words. And there was little wonder in this, for the Tzar was old and fat, and she had lost her heart to Little Fool Ivan.

Angered by her silence the Tzar spoke fiercely. "It is a fact that I am no longer young," he said, "and summer flowers do not bloom again in winter. But for all that I am rich, and I rule over many peoples and a vast dominion. I am a mighty Tzar."

Then the princess spoke. "Never will I wed an old man with grey hair. If you become young again, why then I will consent to be your bride."

"How is it possible for me to grow young again?" asked the Tzar.

"There is a way, O Tzar," answered the princess, "and this is the manner of it. Have two great cauldrons placed in the court-yard; order one to be filled with boiling asses' milk, and one with cold spring water. The man who immerses himself in these two cauldrons one after the other will instantly become young and handsome."

The foolish Tzar bade his servants prepare the cauldrons, for he was minded to make the test, so anxious was he to become young again and handsome.

Then he thought, "What if it does not work? It would be wise that someone else should make the test first." So the Tzar—there was no gratitude in his heart—summoned Little Fool Ivan and told him there was one more task for him to do.

"See the two cauldrons which are set in the courtyard," he said. "One will be filled with boiling liquid and one with cold. When all is ready and the court is assembled you must jump into them one after the other. This is my command."

Poor Little Fool Ivan. When he heard the words of the Tzar he said, "So I must die. Boiled as though I were a fowl or a lump of pork." And sorrowfully he went to the stables to take leave of his little humpback horse.

"You found the sow with the golden bristles, you trapped the mare and the seven stallions, you won the beautiful princess—all for me and to save my life." And he embraced the little horse, kissed its soft nose and stroked its long floppy ears. "But it is all in vain. I am to die a miserable death." And he told the little horse of the Tzar's last order.

"Weep not, little master," said the horse. "Only have faith in me, for our troubles are nearly at an end, and in this case I can serve you well. But listen carefully," he continued, "and do exactly as I say.

"When the Tzar summons you to the courtyard ask for one last favour; that you may bid farewell to your little horse. When I come to you I will blow over the boiling cauldron and it will then be harmless to you. But do not hesitate, jump immediately into the two, one after the other, as the Tzar commanded, and we shall see what we shall see."

Soon Little Fool Ivan was fetched to the courtyard. It was crowded with people; all the court officials were there and the Tzar watched from a balcony. Servants had made huge fires, and the cauldron of milk was bubbling furiously as still more fuel was added.

Silence fell as Ivan appeared. He bowed before the Tzar and cried, "O mighty Tzar, grant me one last favour. Bid them bring my little horse that I may embrace him once more."

The Tzar consented, but told the grooms to make haste. He was impatient for the ceremony to start.

Out came the little humpback horse with his long ears flapping, he seemed to snort as he passed the steaming cauldron, but without anyone noticing he blew a strong breath over the boiling pot, then reaching Ivan, who embraced him, he whispered, "Have courage, and jump quickly."

Ivan leapt boldly into the cauldrons one after the other. He had been a pleasant enough youth before, but now he was so handsome that the crowd cried aloud in amazement.

The Tzar hesitated no longer. He too would be young again and beautiful. He rushed down from the balcony and jumped into the cauldron of boiling milk. But the magic did not work for him, and he died in an instant.

The people then demanded that Little Fool Ivan should be their new Tzar. And the lovely princess willingly agreed to marry him.

The bells rang out; guests came from near and far to the wedding feast, which lasted for three days and three nights.

Tzar Ivan became a mighty ruler, just and wise, and lived long and in happiness with his beautiful Tzaritza. He built a golden stable for the little horse, and never forgot what he owed to him. Indeed, great though he became, Tzar Ivan was never too proud or thought himself too wise to ask for advice from the little humpback horse.

TALES OF LONG AGO

ALI BABA AND THE FORTY THIEVES

In a town in Persia lived two brothers named Cassim and Ali Baba, between whom their father at his death had left what little property he possessed equally divided. Cassim, however, having married the heiress of a rich merchant, became soon after his marriage the owner of a fine shop, together with several pieces of land, and was in consequence, through no effort of his own, the most considerable merchant in the town. Ali Baba, on the other hand, was married to one as poor as himself, and having no other means of gaining a livelihood he used to go every day into the forest to cut wood, and leading therewith the three asses which were his sole stock-in-trade, would then hawk it about the streets for sale.

One day while he was at work within the skirts of the forest, Ali Baba saw advancing towards him across the open a large company of horsemen, and fearing from their appearance that they might be robbers, he left his asses to their own devices and sought safety for himself in the lower branches of a large tree which grew in the close overshadowing of a precipitous rock.

Almost immediately it became evident that this very rock was the goal towards which the troop was bound, for having arrived they alighted instantly from their horses, and took down each man of them a sack which seemed by its weight and form to be filled with gold. There could no longer be any doubt that they were robbers. Ali Baba counted forty of them.

Just as he had done so, the one nearest to him, who seemed to be their chief, advanced towards the rock, and in a low but distinct voice uttered the two words, "Open Sesame!" Immediately the rock opened like a door, the captain and his men passed in, and the rock closed behind them.

For a long while Ali Baba waited, not daring to descend from his hiding-place lest they should come out and catch him in the

Ali Baba and the Forty Thieves

act; but at last, when the waiting had grown almost unbearable, his patience was rewarded, the door in the rock opened and out came the forty men, their captain leading them. When the last of them was through, the captain said, "Shut Sesame!" and immediately the face of the rock closed together as before. Then they all mounted their horses and rode away.

As soon as he felt sure that they were not returning Ali Baba came down from the tree and made his way at once to that part of the rock where he had seen the captain and his men enter. And there at the words "Open Sesame!" a door suddenly revealed itself and opened.

Ali Baba had expected to find a dark and gloomy cavern. Great was his astonishment therefore when he perceived a spacious and vaulted chamber lighted from above through a fissure in the rock; and there spread out before him lay treasures in profusion, bales of merchandise, silks, carpets, brocades, and above all gold and silver lying in loose heaps or in sacks piled one upon another. He did not take long to consider what he should do. Disregarding the silver and the gold that lay loose, he brought to the mouth of the cave as many sacks of gold as he thought his three asses might carry; and having loaded them on and covered them with wood so that they might not be seen, he closed the rock by the utterance of the magic words which he had learned, and departed for the town, a well-satisfied man.

When he got home he drove his asses into a small court, and shutting the gates carefully he took off the covering of wood and carried the sacks in to his wife. She, discovering them to be full of gold, feared that her husband had stolen it, and began sorrowfully to reproach him; but Ali Baba soon put her mind at rest on that score, and having poured all the gold into a great heap upon the floor he sat down at her side to consider how well it looked.

Soon his wife, poor careful body, began counting it over piece by piece. Ali Baba let her go on for a while, but before long the sight set him laughing. "Wife," said he, "you will never make an end of it that way. The best thing to do is to dig a hole and bury it, then we shall be sure that it is not slipping through our fingers." "That will do well enough," said his wife, "but it would be better first to have the measure of it. So while you dig the hole I will go

90

round to Cassim's and borrow a measure small enough to give us an exact reckoning." "Do as you will," answered her husband, "but see that you keep the thing secret."

Off went Ali Baba's wife to her brother-in-law's house. Cassim was from home, so she begged of his wife the loan of a measure, naming for choice the smallest. This set the sister-in-law wondering. Knowing Ali Baba's poverty she was all the more curious to find out for what kind of grain the measure would be used. So before bringing it she covered all the bottom with lard, and giving it to Ali Baba's wife told her to be sure and be quick in returning it. The other, promising to restore it punctually, made haste to get home; and there finding the hole dug for its reception she started to measure the money into it. First she set the measure upon the heap, then she filled it, then she carried it to the hole; and so she continued till the last measure was counted. Then, leaving Ali Baba to finish burying the gold, she carried the measure with all haste to her sister-in-law, returning thanks for the loan.

No sooner was her back turned than Cassim's wife looked at the bottom of the measure, and there to her astonishment she saw sticking to the lard a gold coin. "What?" she cried, her heart filled with envy, "is Ali Baba so rich that he needs a measure for his gold? Where, then, I would know, has the miserable wretch obtained it?"

She waited with impatience for her husband's return, and as soon as he came in she began to jeer at him. "You think yourself rich," said she, "but Ali Baba is richer. You count your gold by the piece, but Ali Baba does not count, he measures it! In comparison to Ali Baba we are but grubs and groundlings!"

Having thus riddled him to the top of her bent in order to provoke his curiosity, she told him the story of the borrowed measure, of her own stratagem, and of its result.

Cassim, instead of being pleased at Ali Baba's sudden prosperity, grew furiously jealous; not a wink could he sleep all night for thinking of it. The next morning before sunrise he went to his brother's house. "Ali Baba," said he, "what do you mean by pretending to be poor when all the time you are scooping up gold by the quart?"

"Brother," said Ali Baba, "explain your meaning."

"My meaning shall be plain!" cried Cassim, displaying the tell-tale coin. "How many more pieces have you like this that my wife found sticking to the bottom of the measure yesterday?"

Ali Baba, perceiving that the intervention of wives had made further concealment useless, told his brother the true facts of the case, and offered him, as an inducement for keeping the secret, an equal share of the treasure.

"That is the least that I have the right to expect," answered Cassim haughtily. "It is further necessary that you should tell me exactly where the treasure lies, that I may, if need be, test the truth of your story, otherwise I shall find it my duty to denounce you to the authorities."

Ali Baba, having a clear conscience, had little fear of Cassim's threats; but out of pure good nature he gave him all the information he desired, not forgetting to instruct him in the words which would give him free passage into the cave and out again.

Cassim, who had thus secured all he had come for, lost no time in putting his project into execution. Intent on possessing himself of all the treasures which yet remained, he set off the next morning before daybreak, taking with him ten mules laden with empty crates. Arrived before the cave, he recalled the words which his brother had taught him; no sooner was "Open Sesame!" said than the door in the rock lay wide for him to pass through, and when he had entered it shut again.

If the simple soul of Ali Baba had found delight in the riches of the cavern, greater still was the exultation of a greedy nature like Cassim's. Intoxicated with the wealth that lay before his eyes, he had no thought but to gather together with all speed as much treasure as the ten mules could carry; and so, having exhausted himself with heavy labour and avaricious excitement, he suddenly found on returning to the door that he had forgotten the key which opened it. Up and down, and in and out through the mazes of his brain he chased the missing word. He remembered it was a grain—barley, and maize, rye, and rice, he thought of them all; but of Sesame never once, because his mind had become dark to the revealing light of heaven. And so the door stayed fast, holding him a prisoner in the cave, where to his fate, undeserving of pity, we leave him.

Ali Baba and the Forty Thieves

Towards noon the robbers returned, and saw, standing about the rock, the ten mules laden with crates. At this they were greatly surprised, and began to search with suspicion amongst the surrounding crannies and undergrowth. Finding no one there, they drew their swords and advanced cautiously towards the cave, where, upon the captain's pronouncement of the magic word, the door immediately fell open. Cassim, who from within had heard the trampling of horses, had now no doubt that the robbers were arrived and that his hour was come. Resolved however to make one last effort at escape, he stood ready by the door; and no sooner had the opening word been uttered than he sprang forth with such violence that he threw the captain to the ground. But his attempt was vain; before he could break through he was mercilessly hacked down by the swords of the robber band.

With their fears thus verified, the robbers anxiously entered the cave to view the traces of its late visitant. There they saw piled by the door the treasure which Cassim had sought to carry away; but while restoring this to its place they failed altogether to detect the earlier loss which Ali Baba had caused them. Reckoning, however, that as one had discovered the secret of entry others also might know of it, they were determined to leave an example for any who might venture thither on a similar errand; and having quartered the body of Cassim they disposed it at the entrance in a manner most calculated to strike horror into the heart of the beholder. Then, closing the door of the cave, they rode away in the search of fresh exploits and plunder.

Meanwhile Cassim's wife had grown very uneasy at her husband's prolonged absence; and at nightfall, unable to endure further suspense, she ran to Ali Baba and, telling him of his brother's secret expedition, entreated him to go out instantly in search of him.

Ali Baba had too kind a heart to refuse or delay comfort to her affliction. Taking with him his three asses he set out immediately for the forest, and as the road was familiar to him he had soon found his way to the door of the cave. When he saw there the traces of blood he became filled with misgiving, but no sooner had he entered than his worst fears were realized. Nevertheless brotherly piety gave him courage. Gathering together the severed remains and wrapping them about with all possible decency, he laid them upon one of the asses; then he loaded the two remaining asses with sacks of gold, and covering them with wood as on the first occasion, made his way back to the town while it was yet early. Leaving his wife to dispose of the treasure borne by the two asses, he led the third to his sister-in-law's house, and knocking quietly so that none of the neighbours might hear, was presently admitted by Morgiana, a female slave whose intelligence and discretion had long been known to him. "Morgiana," said he, "there's trouble on the back of that ass. Can you keep a secret?" And Morgiana's nod satisfied him better than any oath. "Well," said he, "your master's body lies there, and our business now is to bury him honourably as though he had died a natural death. Go and tell your mistress that I want to speak to her."

Morgiana went in to her mistress, and returning presently bade Ali Baba enter. Then leaving him to break to his sister-in-law the news and the sad circumstances of his brother's death, she, with her plan already formed, hastened forth and knocked at the door of the nearest apothecary. As soon as he opened to her she required of him, in trembling agitation certain remedies efficacious against grave disorders, declaring in answer to his questions that her master had been taken suddenly ill. With these she returned home, and her plan of concealment having been explained and agreed upon, much to the satisfaction of Ali Baba, she went forth the next morning to the same apothecary, and with tears in her eyes besought him to supply her in haste with an expensive essence that was only administered to those gravely ill and in the last extremity. Meanwhile the rumour of Cassim's sickness had got abroad; Ali Baba and his wife had been seen coming and going, while Morgiana by her ceaseless activity had made the two days' pretended illness seem like a fortnight: so when a sound of wailing arose within the house all the neighbours concluded without further question that Cassim had died a natural and honourable death.

But Morgiana had now a still more difficult task to perform, it being necessary for the obsequies that the body should be made in some way presentable. So at a very early hour the next morning she went to the shop of a certain merry old cobbler, Baba Mustapha by name, who lived on the other side of the town. Showing him a piece of gold she inquired whether he were ready to earn it by exercising his craft in implicit obedience to her instructions. And when Baba Mustapha sought to know the terms, "First," said she, "you must come with your eyes bandaged; secondly, you must sew what I put before you without asking questions; and thirdly, when you return you must tell nobody."

Mustapha, who had a lively curiosity into other folk's affairs, doggled for a time at the bandaging, and doubted much of his ability to refrain from questions; but having on these considerations secured the doubling of his fee, he promised secrecy readily enough, and taking his cobbler's tackle in hand submitted himself to Morgiana's guidance and set forth. This way and that she led him blindfold, till she had brought him to the house of her deceased master. Then uncovering his eyes in the presence of the dismembered corpse, she bade him get out thread and wax and join the pieces together.

Baba Mustapha accomplished his task according to the compact, asking no questions. When he had done, Morgiana again bandaged his eyes and led him home, and giving him a third piece of gold the more to satisfy him, she bade him good-day and departed.

So in seemliness and without scandal of any kind were the obsequies of the murdered Cassim performed. And when all was ended, seeing that his widow was desolate and his house in need of a protector, Ali Baba with brotherly piety took both the one and the other into his care, marrying his sister-in-law according to Moslem rule, and removing with all his goods and newly acquired treasure to the house which had been his brother's. And having also acquired the shop where Cassim had done business, he put into it his own son, who had already served an apprenticeship to the trade. So, with his fortune well established, let us now leave Ali Baba, and return to the robbers' cave.

Thither, at the appointed time, came the forty robbers, bearing in hand fresh booty; and great was their consternation to discover that not only had the body of Cassim been removed, but a good many sacks of gold as well. It was no wonder that this should trouble them, for so long as anyone could command secret access, the cave was useless as a hiding-place for their wealth. The question was — What could they do to put an end to their present insecurity? After long debate it was agreed that one of their number should go into the town disguised as a traveller and there, mixing with the common people, learn from their report whether there had been recently any case in their midst of sudden prosperity or of sudden death. If such a thing could be discovered, then they could make sure of tracking the man who knew their secret.

Although the penalty for failure was death, one of the robbers at once boldly offered himself for the venture, and having transformed himself by disguise and received the wise counsels and commendations of his fellows, he set out for the town.

Arriving at dawn he began to walk up and down the streets and watch the early stirring of the inhabitants. So, before long, he drew up at the door of Baba Mustapha, who, though old, was already seated at work upon the cobbler's bench. The robber accosted him. "I wonder," said he, "to see a man of your age at work so early. Does not so dull a light strain your eyes?" "Not so much as you might think," answered Baba Mustapha. "Why, it was but the other day at this same hour I saw well enough to stitch up a dead body in a place where it was certainly no lighter." "Stitch up a dead body!" cried the robber in pretended amazement, concealing his joy at his sudden intelligence. "Surely you mean in its winding sheet, for how else can a dead body be stitched?" "No, no," said Mustapha; "what I say I mean; but as it is a secret, I can tell you no more." The robber drew out a piece of gold. "Come," said he, "tell me nothing you do not care to; only show me the house where lay the body that you stitched." Baba Mustapha eyed the gold longingly. "Would that I could," he replied; "but alas! I went to it blindfold." "Well," said the robber, "I have heard that a blind man remembers his road; perhaps, though seeing you might lose it, blindfold you might find it again." Tempted by the offer of a second piece of gold, Baba Mustapha was soon persuaded to make the attempt. "It was here that I started," said he, showing the spot, "and I turned as you see me now." The robber then put a bandage over his eyes, and walked beside him through the streets, partly guiding and partly being led, till of his own accord Baba Mustapha stopped. "It was here," said he. "The door by which I went in should now lie to the right." And he had in fact come exactly opposite to the house which had once been Cassim's, where Ali Baba now dwelt.

The robber, having marked the door with a piece of chalk which he had provided for the purpose, removed the bandage from Mustapha's eyes, and leaving him to his own devices returned with all possible speed to the cave where his comrades were awaiting him.

Soon after the robber and cobbler had parted, Morgiana happened to go out upon an errand, and as she returned she noticed the mark upon the door. "This," she thought, "is not as it should be; either some trick is intended, or there is evil brewing for my master's house." Taking a piece of chalk she put a similar mark upon the five or six doors lying to right and left; and having done this she went home with her mind satisfied, saying nothing.

In the meantime the robbers had learned from their companion the success of his venture. Greatly elated at the thought of the vengeance so soon to be theirs, they formed a plan for entering the city in a manner that should arouse no suspicion among the inhabitants. Passing in by twos and threes, and by different routes, they came together to the market-place at an appointed time, while the captain and the robber who had acted as spy made their way alone to the street in which the marked door was to be found. Presently, just as they had expected, they perceived a door with the mark on it. "That is it!" said the robber; but as they continued walking so as to avoid suspicion, they came upon another and another, till, before they were done, they had passed six in succession. So alike were the marks that the spy, though he swore he had made but one, could not tell which it was. Seeing that the design had failed, the captain returned to the market-place, and having passed the word for his troop to go back in the same way as they had come, he himself set the example of retreat.

When they were all reassembled in the forest, the captain explained how the matter had fallen, and the spy, acquiescing in his own condemnation, kneeled down and received the stroke of the executioner.

But as it was still necessary for the safety of all that so great a trespass and theft should not pass unavenged, another of the band, undeterred by the fate of his comrade, volunteered upon the same conditions to prosecute the quest wherein the other had failed. Coming by the same means to the house of Ali Baba, he set upon the door, at a spot not likely to be noticed, a mark in red chalk to distinguish it clearly from those which were already marked in white. But even this precaution failed of its end. Morgiana, whose eye nothing could escape, noticed the red mark at the first time of passing, and dealt with it just as she had done with the previous one. So when the robbers came, hoping this time to light upon the door without fail, they found not one but six all similarly marked with red.

When the second spy had received the due reward of his blunder, the captain considered how by trusting to others he had come to lose two of his bravest followers, so the third attempt he determined to conduct in person. Having found his way to Ali Baba's door, as the two others had done by the aid of Baba Mustapha, he did not set any mark upon it, but examined it so carefully that he could not in future mistake it. He then returned to the forest and communicated to his band the plan which he had formed. This was to go into the town in the disguise of an oil-merchant, bearing with him upon nineteen mules thirty-eight large leather jars, one of which, as a sample, was to be full of oil, but all the others empty. In these he purposed to conceal the thirty-seven robbers to which his band was now reduced, and so to convey his full force to the scene of action in such a manner as to arouse no suspicion till the signal for vengeance should be given.

Within a couple of days he had secured the mules and jars that were necessary, and having disposed of his troop according to the pre-arranged plan, he drove his train of well-laden mules to the gates of the city, through which he passed just before sunset. Proceeding thence to Ali Baba's house, and arriving as it fell dark, he was about to knock and crave a lodging for the night, when he perceived Ali Baba at the door enjoying the fresh air after supper. Addressing him in tones of respect, "Sir," said he, "I have brought my oil a great distance to sell tomorrow in the market; and at this late hour, being a stranger, I know not where to seek for a shelter. If it is not troubling you too much, allow me to stable my beasts here for the night."

The captain's voice was now so changed from its accustomed

tone of command, that Ali Baba, though he had heard it before, did not recognize it. Not only did he grant the stranger's request for bare accommodation, but as soon as the unloading and stabling of the mules had been accomplished, he invited him to stay no longer in the outer court but enter the house as his guest. The captain, whose plans this proposal somewhat disarranged, endeavoured to excuse himself by a pretended reluctance to give trouble; but since Ali Baba would take no refusal he was forced at last to yield, and to submit with apparent complaisance to an entertainment which the hospitality of his host extended to a late hour.

When they were about to retire for the night, Ali Baba went into the kitchen to speak to Morgiana; and the captain of the robbers, on the pretext of going to look after his mules, slipped out into the yard where the oil jars were standing in line. Passing from jar to jar he whispered into each, "When you hear a handful of pebbles fall from the window of the chamber where I am lodged, then cut your way out of the jar and make ready, for the time will have come." He then returned to the house, where Morgiana came with a light and conducted him to his chamber.

Now Ali Baba, before going to bed, had said to Morgiana, "To-morrow at dawn I am going to the baths; let my bathing-linen be put ready, and see that the cook has some good broth prepared for me against my return." Having therefore led the guest up to his chamber, Morgiana returned to the kitchen and ordered Abdallah the cook to put on the pot for the broth. Suddenly while she was skimming it, the lamp went out, and, on searching, she found there was no more oil in the house. At so late an hour no shop would be open, yet somehow the broth had to be made, and that could not be done without a light. "As for that," said Abdallah, seeing her perplexity, "why trouble yourself? There is plenty of oil out in the yard." "Why, to be sure!" said Morgiana, and sending Abdallah to bed so that he might be up in time to wake his master on the morrow, she took the oil-can herself and went out into the court. As she approached the jar which stood nearest, she heard a voice within say, "Is it time?"

To one of Morgiana's intelligence an oil-jar that spoke was an object of even more suspicion than a chalk-mark on a door, and in an instant she apprehended what danger for her master and his family might lie concealed around her. Understanding well enough that an oil-jar which asked a question required an answer, she replied quick as thought and without the least sign of perturbation, "Not yet, but presently." And thus she passed from jar to jar, thirty-seven in all, giving the same answer, till she came to the one which contained the oil.

The situation was now clear to her. Aware of the source from which her master had acquired his wealth, she guessed at once that, in extending shelter to the oil-merchant, Ali Baba had in fact admitted to his house the robber captain and his band. On the instant her resolution was formed. Having filled the oil-can she returned to the kitchen; there she lighted the lamp and then, taking a large kettle, went back once more to the jar which contained the oil. Filling the kettle she carried it back to the kitchen, and putting under it a great fire of wood had soon brought it to the boil. Then taking it in hand once more, she went out into the yard and poured into each jar in turn a sufficient quantity of the boiling oil to scald its occupant to death.

She then returned to the kitchen, and having made Ali Baba's broth, put out the fire, blew out the lamp, and sat down by the window to watch.

Before long the captain of the robbers awoke from the short sleep which he had allowed himself, and finding that all was silent in the house, he rose softly and opened the window. Below stood the oil-jars; gently into their midst he threw the handful of pebbles agreed on as a signal; but from the oil-jars came no answer. He threw a second and a third time; yet though he could hear the pebbles falling among the jars, there followed only the silence of the dead. Wondering whether his band had fled leaving him in the lurch, or whether they were asleep, he grew uneasy, and descending in haste, made his way into the court. As he approached the first jar a smell of burning and hot oil assailed his nostrils, and looking within he beheld in rigid contortion the dead body of his comrade. In every jar the same sight presented itself, till he came to the one which had contained the oil. There, in what was missing, the means and manner of his companions' death were made clear to him. Aghast at the discovery and awake to the danger that now threatened him, he did not delay an instant, but forcing the garden-gate, and thence climbing from wall to wall, he made his escape out of the city.

When Morgiana, who had remained all this time on the watch, was assured of his final departure, she put her master's bath-linen ready and went to bed well satisfied with her day's work.

The next morning Ali Baba, awakened by his slave, went to the baths before daybreak. On his return he was greatly surprised to find that the merchant was gone, leaving his mules and oil-jars behind him. He inquired of Morgiana the reason. "You will find the reason," said she, "if you look into the first jar you come to." Ali Baba did so, and, seeing a man, started back with a cry. "Do not be afraid," said Morgiana, "he is dead and harmless; and so are all the others whom you will find if you look further."

As Ali Baba went from one jar to another, finding always the same sight of horror within, his knees trembled under him; and when he came at last to the one empty oil-jar, he stood for a time motionless, turning upon Morgiana eyes of wonder and inquiry. "And what," he said then, "has become of the merchant?" "To tell you that," said Morgiana, "will be to tell you the whole story; you will be better able to hear it if you have your broth first."

But the curiosity of Ali Baba was far too great; he would not be kept waiting. So without further delay she gave him the whole history, so far as she knew it, from beginning to end; and by her intelligent putting of one thing against another, she left him at last in no possible doubt as to the source and nature of the conspiracy which her quick wits had so happily defeated. "And now, dear master," she said in conclusion, "continue to be on your guard, for though all these are dead, one remains alive; and he, if I mistake not, is the captain of the band, and for that reason the more formidable and the more likely to cherish the hope of vengeance."

When Morgiana had done speaking Ali Baba clearly perceived that he owed to her not merely the protection of his property but life itself. His heart was full of gratitude. "Do not doubt," he said, "that before I die I will reward you as you deserve; and as an immediate proof from this moment I give you your liberty."

This token of his approval filled Morgiana's heart with delight, but she had no intention of leaving so kind a master, even had she been sure that all danger was now over. The immediate question which next presented itself was how to dispose of the bodies. Luckily at the far end of the garden stood a thick grove of trees, and under these Ali Baba was able to dig a large trench without attracting the notice of his neighbours. Here the remains of the thirty-seven robbers were laid side by side, the trench was filled again, and the ground made level. As ior the mules, since Ali Baba had no use for them, he sent them, one or two at a time, to the market to be sold.

Meanwhile the robber captain had fled back to the forest. He was mortified beyond measure at the failure of his plan, and the sudden extinction of his band, and he vowed to take vengeance on Ali Baba for the death of his companions.

Thus resolved, at an early hour the next day, he assumed a disguise suitable to his purpose, and going to the town took lodging in a khan. Entering into conversation with his host he inquired whether anything of interest had happened recently in the town; but the other, though full of gossip, had nothing to tell him concerning the matter in which he was most interested, for Ali Baba, having to conceal from all the source of his wealth, had also to be silent as to the dangers in which it involved him.

The captain then inquired where there was a shop for hire; and hearing of one that suited him, he came to terms with the owner, and before long had furnished it with all kinds of rich stuffs and carpets and jewellery which he brought by degrees with great secrecy from the cave.

Now this shop happened to be opposite to that which had belonged to Cassim and was now occupied by the son of Ali Baba; so before long the son and the new-comer, who had assumed the name of Cogia Houssain, became acquainted; and as the youth had good looks, kind manners, and a sociable disposition, it was not long before the acquaintance became intimate.

Cogia Houssain did all he could to seal the pretended friendship, the more so as it had not taken him long to discover how the young man and Ali Baba were related; so, plying him constantly with small presents and acts of hospitality, he forced on him the obligation of making some return.

Ali Baba's son, however, had not at his lodging sufficient accom-

Ali Baba and the Forty Thieves

modation for entertainment; he therefore told his father of the difficulty in which Cogia Houssain's favours had placed him, and Ali Baba with great willingness at once offered to arrange matters. "My son," said he, "tomorrow being a holiday, all shops will be closed; then do you after dinner invite Cogia Houssain to walk with you; and as you return bring him this way and beg him to come in. That will be better than a formal invitation, and Morgiana shall have a supper prepared for you."

This proposal was exactly what Ali Baba's son could have wished, so on the morrow he brought Cogia Houssain to the door as if by accident, and stopping, invited him to enter.

Cogia Houssain, who saw his object thus suddenly attained, began by showing pretended reluctance, but Ali Baba himself coming to the door, pressed him in the most kindly manner to enter, and before long had conducted him to the table, where food stood prepared.

But there an unlooked-for difficulty arose. Wicked though he might be, the robber captain was not so impious as to eat the salt of the man he intended to kill. He therefore began with many apologies to excuse himself; and when Ali Baba sought to know the reason, "Sir," said he, "I am sure that if you knew the cause of my resolution you would approve of it. Suffice it to say that I have made it a rule to eat of no dish that has salt in it. How then can I sit down at your table if I must reject everything that is set before me?"

"If that is your scruple," said Ali Baba, "it shall soon be satisfied," and he sent orders to the kitchen that no salt was to be put into any of the dishes presently to be served to the newly arrived guest. "Thus," said he to Cogia Houssain, "I shall still have the honour, to which I have looked forward, of returning to you under my own roof the hospitality you have shown to my son."

Morgiana, who was just about to serve supper, received the order with some discontent. "Who," she said, "is this difficult person that refuses to eat salt? He must be a curiosity worth looking at." So when the saltless courses were ready to be set upon the table, she herself helped to carry the dishes. No sooner had she set eyes on Cogia Houssain than she recognized him in spite of his disguise; and observing his movements with great attention she saw that he had a dagger concealed beneath his robe. "Ah!" she said to herself, "here is reason enough! For who will eat salt with the man he means to murder? But he shall not murder my master if I can prevent it."

Now Morgiana knew that the most favourable opportunity for the robber captain to carry out his design would be after the courses had been withdrawn, and when Ali Baba and his son and guest were alone together over their wine, which indeed was the very project that Cogia Houssain had formed. Going forth, therefore, in haste, she dressed herself as a dancer, assuming the head-dress and mask suitable for the character. Then she fastened a silver girdle about her waist, and hung upon it a dagger of the same material. Thus equipped, she said to Abdallah the cook, "Take your tabor and let us go in and give an entertainment in honour of our master's guest."

So Abdallah took his tabor, and played Morgiana into the hall. As soon as she had entered she made a low curtsy, and stood awaiting orders. Then Ali Baba, seeing that she wished to perform in his guest's honour, said kindly, "Come in, Morgiana, and show Cogia Houssain what you can do."

Immediately Abdallah began to beat upon his tabor and sing an air for Morgiana to dance to; and she, advancing with much grace and propriety of deportment, began to move through several figures, performing them with the ease and facility which none but the most highly practised can attain to. Then, for the last figure of all, she drew out the dagger and, holding it in her hand, danced a dance which excelled all that had preceded it in the surprise and change and quickness and dexterity of its movements. Now she presented the dagger at her own breast, now at one of the on-lookers; but always in the act of striking she drew back. At length, as though out of breath, she snatched his instrument from Abdallah with her left hand, and, still holding the dagger in her right, advanced the hollow of the tabor towards her master, as is the custom of dancers when claiming their fee. Ali Baba threw in a piece of gold; his son did likewise. Then advancing it in the same manner towards Cogia Houssain, who was feeling for his purse, she struck under it, and before he knew had plunged her dagger deep into his heart.

Ali Baba and his son, seeing their guest fall dead, cried out in horror at the deed. "Wretch!" exclaimed Ali Baba, "what ruin and shame hast thou brought on us?" "Nay," answered Morgiana, "it is not your ruin but your life that I have secured; look and convince yourself what man was this who refused to eat salt with you!" So saying, she tore off the dead robber's disguise, showing the dagger concealed below, and the face which her master now for the first time recognized.

Ali Baba's gratitude to Morgiana for thus preserving his life a second time, knew no bounds. He took her in his arms and embraced her as a daughter. "Now," said he, "the time is come when I must fulfil my debt; and how better can I do it than by marrying you to my son?" This proposition, far from proving unwelcome to the young man, did but confirm an inclination already formed. A few days later the nuptials were celebrated with great joy and solemnity, and the union thus auspiciously commenced was productive of as much happiness as lies within the power of mortals to secure.

As for the robbers' cave, it remained the secret possession of Ali Baba and his descendants; and using their good fortune with equity and moderation, they rose to high office in the city and were held in great honour by all who knew them.

BEOWULF AND GRENDEL

Hrothgar's Coast Warden, sitting his horse on the cliff top northward of Heorot, saw a strange vessel running in from the open sea, between the high headlands at the mouth of the fjord. A war-galley, long and slim and swift; and the light blinked on the painted shields hung along her bulwarks and the grey battle-gear of the men who swung to her oars. Her square striped sail fell slack as the headland took the wind from it, and then came rattling down, and urged by her rowers she headed like some eager many-legged sea creature for the low shelving beach where the cliffs dropped at the head of the fjord.

Frowning, the Coast Warden wheeled his horse, and touching his heel to its flank, urged it into the cliff path that looped down in the same direction. He came out through the furze and the salt-burned bush-tangle above the shore, just as the strange war-boat came lightly in through the shallows. Her crew unshipped their oars and sprang overboard into the white oar-thresh while it still foamed along her sides, and now they were running her up the shingle to strand on the tide-line.

Fifteen of them, the Coast Warden counted; and the sunlight sparkled on their weapons as they swung their painted linden shields clear of the bulwarks; and yet they had not the wolf-pack look of a raiding band. Again he touched his heel to his horse's flank and, spear in hand, rode down into their midst, where they turned at the sound of hooves and stood waiting for his coming, gathered about the upreared dragon prow of their vessel.

To one who was clearly the leader among them, a very tall man whose eyes were coloured like deep water on a cloudy day, the Coast Warden spoke boldly, yet courteously enough. "Who are you, strangers from across the sea, and what purpose brings you to this landfall on the Danish shore? You come in war array, armed as for battle, yet you have not the look of those who come to burn farms and carry off women and cattle."

"In truth, though we come in war array, the battle that we seek is not with the Danish folk," the tall man said. "As to who we are—I am Beowulf, sister's-son to Hygelac, King of the Geats, and these with me are my sword-brothers and hearth-companions. As to our purpose—a few days since, word came to Hygelac's Court that Hrothgar of the Danes was in need of champions to rid him of the monster that walks his hall at night; and so we are come, following the Whale's Road southward across the grey Baltic from our own strand."

For a long moment, while the surf creamed on the shore, the Coast Warden sat his horse and looked at them, his eyes narrowed under his brows; he was old and a judge of men. Then he nodded. "So. It is long and long that Hrothgar and all his folk have waited for such champions. Come then, and I will set you on your way to the King's hall."

"First we must make all secure here," said Beowulf, and he

reached up his hand and set it on the swell of the painted dragon-prow above him, caressingly as though it were a living thing. "Horse or vessel should be tended first of all things at a journey's end."

"Have no fear for your proud vessel. I will send trustworthy men of my own to make all fast with a barricade of oars against the high tide." The old man was eager now. "If you are indeed the champions you seem, let Hrothgar my lord wait no longer, for he has waited over long already for help," and he pointed along a rough track that wound up from the beach through the furze and the hazel thickets. "See, our way lies yonder."

In single file, for the track was too narrow to walk abreast, Beowulf and his comrades followed the old Warden on his horse up from the head of the fjord, a grey mailed serpent of men, the forged rings of their battle-sarks ringing as they moved. On the crest of the ridge where the wind-shaped trees fell back, the track changed abruptly into a paved road, and there they checked, with the sea wind humming against their mailed shoulders. Behind them was the way home, the fjord running out between its nesses to the open sea, and the war-boat lying like a basking seal among the brown sea-wrack and the driftwood on the high tide line. Ahead of them lay the unknown and the hazard that they had come to seek. From their feet the land dropped away into a shallow vale, then rose again to sombre moors inland, and a mile off, in the trough of the vale between the coast and the moors, Beowulf, narrowing his eyes into the sunlight, could see a great hall rising among a scatter of lesser roofs, the green and brown of tilled land, the darker dapple of orchard trees. And straight towards the hall, purposeful as the flight of an arrow, ran the paved road on which he stood.

"Yonder is Heorot," said the Coast Warden's voice in his ear. "The road will take you to the very door sill. I must be away back to the coast, but do you go forward now, my friends, and have no fear for your ship; she shall be well tended." And without another word he swung his horse in a half-circle and was gone, trampling away down the rough track behind them. And Beowulf and his companions went forward alone.

Down from the high coast-wise ridge they strode, into the green pasture lands where the cattle and horses grazed, through the cornland where the young barley was already a mist of green over the dark earth, between the first heather-thatched homesteads of the settlement, each with its bee skeps along the wall and its few apple trees, where children and dogs and lean pigs were playing together, and women grinding corn or spinning in their doorways looked up to watch the strangers pass.

It all seemed peaceful enough—now, with the sun still high in the sky.

In the midst of the settlement the roof of the King's hall rose higher and higher as they drew towards it; Heorot the Hart, heather-thatched like all the rest, but with the gilded antlers on the gable ends proudly up-tossed towards the sky. Straight to the foreporch doorway ran the paved road; and up it, their war-gear sounding on them as the feathers of wild swans sound in flight, strode the fifteen Geats.

In the doorway one of the household thanes stood leaning on a spear; a dark man with beads of yellow sea-washed amber round his neck. His gaze was upon them as they came to a halt before him; and he asked, as the Coast Warden had asked, "Who are you, strangers who come in war-harness to the threshold of Hrothgar the King? And what is it that you seek here?"

"As to who we are—I am sister's-son to Hygelac, King of the Geats, and these with me are my sword-brothers and hearth-companions," Beowulf replied, as he had done before. "As to what we seek here – we would have word with Hrothgar the King, for our business is with him."

"Wait then, and I will carry your name to Hrothgar," said the man, and turned back into the fire-flickered shadows behind him, from which came men's voices and the smell of roast meat.

Beowulf and his comrades sat down on the guest-bench in the sunlight before the door, but they had only a short while to wait before the door-thane returned, and at his bidding they stacked their shields and ashen spears against the wall, and followed him into the hall where Hrothgar's house-thanes sat at meat.

Great and splendid indeed was Heorot to the gaze of Beowulf as he stepped across the door sill on to the many-coloured flag-stones of the floor. Down the midst of the hall the fires blazed on their three hearths, and the smoke curled upwards to find its way out through the openings in the roof high overhead, and through the drifting haze that hung about the place he saw the warriors at the long tables, with mead horns and boar flesh and huge piles of barley cakes before them; saw too the walls and roof-trees rich with worked hangings and ornaments of white walrus ivory, and the shields and spears of the warriors hung above the mead benches.

Hrothgar's High Seat was on a raised dais at the far end, and so the Geatish warriors must walk the full length of the place, between the long trestle tables, to come to him; and all tongues fell silent and every eye was turned upon them, but especially upon their tall leader, as they passed.

At the step of the dais Beowulf halted and stood proudly confronting Hrothgar; and the Danish King leaned forward, hands clenched on the foreposts of his great carved seat, to stare down at him.

From the farmost fringes of his childhood's memory Beowulf recalled the stern yet kindly features. But Hrothgar was old now, the lines on his face were bitten deep as sword-cuts by years of grief, and the beard that jutted over the broad goldwork collar at his throat was grey as a badger's pelt.

"So it is true," the old man said broodingly, after a long silence. "I scarce believed . . . But there is that in your face that I should know again if you stood among a hundred warriors; aye, though you stood no higher at the shoulder, when last I saw you, than my favourite hound. My heart leapt up within me when Wulfnoth my door-thane brought word that Beowulf, sister's-son to the Geatish King, sat waiting on my guest-bench to have speech with me as your father had done so many years ago. Most joyfully are you welcome, you and your comrades with you. But tell me what brings you here to my threshold?"

"Seafaring men brought to Geatland word of the evil that has fallen upon the Danish King and his folk; and so we come, I and my sword-brothers, to offer our service and our strength against the thing that walks Heorot in the dark. Men say that I have the strength of thirty warriors in my grip." Beowulf raised his arms as he spoke, and held them out to the old King in a gesture that was half proud and half pleading. "And it is yours, for my father's sake. Give to me and my comrades leave to sleep in your hall tonight."

Hrothgar bent his face into his hands, then he raised it again, and looked long and earnestly at Beowulf who stood tall as a spear in his grey war-gear before him. "So you have come for friendship's sake," he said at last, "for the sake of the bond that was between your father and myself when the world was young. Yet think before it is too late; think of the hideous end that has come to every man who has stood in this place to pit his strength and courage against the Death-Shadow-in-the-Dark. Grendel's strength cannot be measured even against the strength of thirty men, for it is beyond the measuring of mortal strength. They also were young and strong, those other champions who have stood here before you, but youth and strength did not avail them. In the name of the old friendship that brought you here I bid you think, and be very sure, before the time for thinking is past."

"We have thought, all of us, and we are content to abide whatever the night may bring," Beowulf said. "The outcome must be as Wyrd who weaves the fates of men may choose."

The light of great hope kindled slowly in the King's face, and he straightened himself in the high carved seat. "So be it, then: I accept the aid that you bring me. Sleep in my hall tonight, but meanwhile do you and those who come with you feast with high hearts among my thanes."

At this, a clamour of voices, fiercely joyful, arose from the warriors who had held their listening silence while Beowulf and the King spoke together; and room and welcome were made for the strangers on the crowded benches. Beowulf found himself sitting between Hrothgar's two young sons. Steaming boar's flesh and eel pie were set before him and a great mead horn thrust into his hands, and the feasting in Heorot roared up like a fire when dry birch bark is flung on to it.

The feasting continued, and men grew fiercely merry, and the harper stood up to make music beside the King's hearth. Then the hangings of embroidered stuff that closed the doorway to the women's quarters were drawn aside, and a woman stood there with others behind her, a tall woman in a crimson robe, dark-eyed and dark-haired, with royal goldwork about her head, and in her hands a great golden cup.

She had no part with Hrothgar in Beowulf's early memory, for she was a second wife, and much younger than her lord, but looking at her, he knew that she must be Wealhtheow the Queen. She came forward, her women behind her, and the cheerful uproar lulled at her coming. She carried the golden cup first to Hrothgar, where he sat in his High Seat, saying in a clear voice that reached to the farthest end of the hall, "We have heard, even in the women's quarters, of the champions from across the sea who feast in Heorot this evening; and we have heard the brave purpose of their coming. Surely now our sorrows are almost over; therefore drink, my dear lord, and let your heart be lightened."

And when the King had drunk, she carried the cup from one to another of the warriors, Geat and Dane alike, all down the benches, while one of her women coming behind with the mead jar refilled for her as often as the cup grew low. Last of all she came to Beowulf where he sat as guest of honour between her two sons. "Greeting, and joy be to you, Beowulf, and all the thanks of our hearts, that you come so valiantly to our aid."

Beowulf rose to his feet and took the cup as she held it out to him. "Valour is a word to use when the battle is over," he said, smiling. "Give us your thanks, great Queen, when we have done the thing which we came to do. But this at least I promise you, that if we fail to rid you of the monster, we shall not live to carry home our shields." And throwing back his head, he drained the cup and gave it again into her hands.

But now the shadows were gathering in the corners of the hall, and as the daylight faded, a shadow seemed to gather on the hearts of all men there, a shadow that was all too long familiar to the Danes. Then Hrothgar rose in his High Seat, and called Beowulf to him again.

"Soon it will be dusk," he said, when the young Geat stood before him. "And yet again the time of dread comes upon Heorot. You are still determined upon this desperate venture?"

"I am not wont to change my purpose without cause," Beowulf said, "and those with me are of a like mind, or they would not have taken ship with me from Geatland in the first place."

"So. Keep watch, then. If you prevail in the combat before you, you shall have such reward from me as never yet heroes had from a King. I pray to the All-Father that when the light grows again out of tonight's dark, you may stand here to claim it. Heorot is yours until morning." And he turned and walked out through the postern door, a tall old man stooping under the burden of his own height, to his sleeping quarters, where Wealhtheow the Queen had gone before him.

All up and down the hall men were taking leave of each other, dwindling away to their own sleeping-places for the night. The thralls set back the benches and stacked the trestle boards against the gable-walls, and spread out straw-filled bolsters and warm wolfskin rugs for the fifteen warriors. Then they too were gone, and Heorot was left to the band of Geats, and the dreadful thing whose shadow was already creeping towards them through the dark.

"Bar the doors," Beowulf said, when the last footsteps of the last thrall had died away. "Bars will not keep him out, but at least they may give us some warning of his coming."

And when two of them had done his bidding, and the seldom-used bars were in their sockets, there was nothing more that could be done.

For a little, as the last fire sank lower, they stood about it, sometimes looking at each other, sometimes into the glowing embers, seldom speaking. Not one of them had much hope that he would see the daylight again, yet none repented of having followed their leader upon the venture. One by one, the fourteen lay down in their harness, with their swords beside them. But Beowulf stripped off his battle-sark and gave it with his sword and boar-crested helmet to Waegmund his kinsman and the dearest to him of all his companions, for he knew that mortal weapons were of no use against the Troll-kind; such creatures must be mastered, if they could be mastered at all, by a man's naked strength, and the red courage of his heart.

In the darkest hour of the spring night Grendel came to Heorot as he had come so many times before, up from his lair and over the high moors, through the mists that seemed to travel with him under the pale moon; Grendel, the Night-Stalker, the Death-Shadow. He came to the foreporch and snuffed about it, and smelled the man-smell, and found that the door which had stood unlatched for him so long was barred and bolted. Snarling in rage that any man should dare attempt to keep him out, he set the flat of his talon-tipped hands against the timbers and burst them in.

Dark as it was, the hall seemed to fill with a monstrous shadow at his coming; a shadow in which Beowulf, half springing up, then holding himself in frozen stillness, could make out no shape nor clear outline save two eyes filled with a wavering greenish flame.

The ghastly corpse-light of his own eyes showed Grendel the shapes of men as it seemed sleeping, and he did not notice among them one who leaned up on his elbow. Laughing in his throat, he reached out and grabbed young Hondscio who lay nearest to him, and almost before his victim had time to cry out, tore him limb from limb and drank the warm blood. Then, while the young warrior's dying shriek still hung upon the air, he reached for another. But this time his hand was met and seized in a grasp such as he had never felt before; a grasp that had in it the strength of thirty men. And for the first time he who had brought fear to so many caught the taste of it himself, knowing that at last he had met his match and maybe his master.

Beowulf leapt from the sleeping-bench and grappled him in the darkness; and terror broke over Grendel in full force, the terror of a wild animal trapped; so that he thought no more of his hunting but only of breaking the terrible hold upon his arm and flying back into the night and the wilderness, and he howled and bellowed as he struggled for his freedom. Beowulf set his teeth and summoned all his strength and tightened his grip until the sinews cracked; and locked together they reeled and staggered up and down the great hall. Trestles and sleeping-benches went over with crash on crash as they strained this way and that, trampling even through the last red embers of the dying fire; and the very walls seemed to groan and shudder as though the stout timbers would burst apart. And all the while Grendel snarled and shrieked and Beowulf fought in silence save for his gasping breaths.

Outside, the Danes listened in horror to the turmoil that seemed as though it must split Heorot asunder; and within, the Geats had sprung from their sleeping-benches sword in hand, forgetful of their powerlessness against the Troll-kind, but in the dark, lit only by stray gleams of bale-fire from the monster's eyes, they dared not strike for fear of slaying their leader, and when one or other of them did contrive to get in a blow, the sword blade glanced off Grendel's charmed hide as though he were sheathed in dragon scales.

At last, when the hall was wrecked to the walls, the Night-Stalker gathered himself for one last despairing effort to break free. Beowulf's hold was as fierce as ever; yet none the less the two figures burst apart—and Grendel with a frightful shriek staggered to the doorway and through it, and fled wailing into the night, leaving his arm and shoulder torn from the roots in the hero's still unbroken grasp.

Beowulf sank down sobbing for breath on a shattered bench, and his fellows came crowding round him with torches rekindled at the scattered embers of the fire; and together they looked at the thing he held across his knees. "Not even the Troll-kind could live half a day with a wound such as that upon them," one of them said; and Waegmund agreed. "He is surely dead as though he lay here among the benches."

"Hondscio is avenged, at all events," said Beowulf. "Let us hang up this thing for a trophy, and a proof that we do not boast idly as the wind blows over."

So in triumph they nailed up the huge scaly arm on one of the roof beams above the High Seat of Hrothgar.

The first thin light of day was already washing over the moors, and almost before the grizzly thing was securely in place the Danes returned to Heorot. They came thronging in to beat Beowulf in joyful acclaim upon his bruised and claw-marked shoulders, and gaze up in awe at the huge arm whose taloned fingers seemed even now to be striving to claw down the roof beam. Many of them called for their horses and followed the blood trail that Grendel had left in his flight up through the tilled land and over the moors until they came to the deep sea-inlet where the monster had his lair, and saw the churning waves between the rocks all fouled and boiling with blood. Meanwhile others set all things on foot for a day of rejoicing, and the young men wrestled together and raced their horses against each other, filling the day with their merry-making, while the King's harper walked to and fro by himself under the apple trees, making a song in praise of Beowulf ready for the evening's feasting which this night would not end when darkness fell.

And Hrothgar and his Queen came from their own place, with his chief thanes and her women behind them, to hear the story of the night's battle and gaze up at the bloody trophy nailed to the roof beam.

THE BIRTH OF PRYDERI

Now it happened in the third year of the marriage of Pwyll prince of Dyfed, and lord over south-west Wales, and Rhiannon, daughter of Hefeydd the Old, that the people of the land came to feel great heaviness of heart because the throne of Dyfed was still without an heir. "Lord," they said, "we are much troubled lest after your day we shall not enjoy the rule of so pleasant a man as you. Truth to tell, you cannot last for ever, and it is our advice that you set aside the wife you have and take another by whom you may have a son to follow you."

"There is a time for all things, friends," Pwyll reproved them, "and many a chance may yet befall. Let us put off this talk for a twelvemonth and a day, and maybe I shall then submit to your counsel."

Before the end of that time a son was born to Pwyll and Rhiannon, and all the countryside offered up prayers and rejoicing. The night he was born six women were brought into the queen's chamber at Arberth, to keep watch over the mother and child. For the first part of the night they kept good watch, but towards midnight they grew drowsy, and soon they were all asleep. It was cockcrow when they awoke, and when they looked in the place where they laid the boy to sleep, there was no sign of him. "Alas," they cried, "the boy is lost, and our lives shall be forfeit unless we find him." They sat down to think what might be done in the matter, and this is what they decided on. In the chamber near the bed there was a couched stag-hound and her pups, so

they agreed to kill some of the pups and smear the blood on Rhiannon's face and hands, and throw the bones before her, and swear that she herself had destroyed her son. "For we are six to one," they said, "and she will be helpless against our insistence."

No sooner had they agreed to this than the lady Rhiannon awoke. "Ladies," she asked, "where is my son? I cannot wait to see him."

"Alas," they said, "lady, do not ask us for your son. Look, we are black and blue from struggling with you, and in all our lives we never saw a woman of such strength and violence. We did what we could, but it was to no purpose, and it is best that you should hear at once the crime you have committed. Lady, you have destroyed your son."

The lady Rhiannon knew well that they were lying. "Poor creatures," she said, "it is your fear that makes you accuse me. Take my promise that I will protect you if you tell the truth."

"Faith," they replied, "it is not for us to suffer hurt for your sake, queen and lady though you are. We say again that you destroyed your son last night."

"Poor wretches," she said a second time, "it would be far better for me to know the truth." But for all her words, whether fair-spoken or pitiful, she received the same answer from the women as before.

Then Pwyll arose, and his war-band and the hosts, and the disaster which had befallen the kingdom was made known to them. The chief men assembled together, and they urged Pwyll that he should set Rhiannon aside, or have her put to death, because she had wrought so monstrous a crime. But the answer they received from Pwyll was this: "Once before you asked me to set aside my wife, and time proved you wrong. I think it will prove you wrong again. I will not put her away, and the only punishment she shall suffer is that which our law enjoins for a case unproved."

"Then let her do penance," said the nobles. "We will be content with that."

And because Rhiannon preferred doing penance to wrangling with the women, and because the women were resolute in their lie, she took on her penance. This was to remain in that court at Arberth till the end of seven years, and to sit every day near the horse-block which was outside the gate, and to relate her story to every new-comer who might be expected not to know it; and to everyone who would permit her to do so, she must offer to carry guest and stranger on her back to the court. And in this fashion the years passed by.

At this same time the lord Teyrnon was ruler over Gwent Is-Coed. There was no better man alive than he. He had a great treasure in his house, by way of a mare; she was the handsomest mare in the kingdom. Every May-eve she dropped a foal, but what became of it no one knew. One night (and it was the very night that Rhiannon's son was born) Teyrnon talked this over with his wife. "It is very slack of us," he reminded her, "to let our mare foal each year and have never a foal to show for her pains. Tonight is May-eve, and shame on my beard if I do not discover what evil destiny it is that snatches away the colts."

He had the mare brought inside the building, and with his sword about him he settled down to watch for the night. Early in the night the mare cast a colt which was unusually large and handsome, and strong enough to stand up on the spot. Teyrnon rose to his feet and was remarking the sturdiness and good colouring of the colt when he heard a great commotion, and after the commotion he saw a huge claw coming in through the window of the house and seizing the colt by the mane. Teyrnon instantly drew his sword and took aim at the claw, and struck off the arm at the elbow, so that that much of the arm together with the colt fell back inside the house with him. A loud scream instantly mingled with the commotion, and he flung open the door and rushed outside, but because the night was black and starless he saw nothing to pursue. Besides, he remembered that he had left the house open behind him, and thought it prudent to return. And there at the door he found an infant boy in swaddling clothes, with a sheet of brocaded silk wrapped round him. He took up the boy, marvelling, and carried him in to his wife.

"Lady," he asked, "are you asleep?"

"I was asleep," she made answer, "but I awoke as you came in."

"Wife," he said, "we have always wanted a son, and now, if you will have him, here is a boy for us." He went on to tell her the whole story, and her heart grew tender towards the child, and they knew by the sheet of brocaded silk and by the whiteness of his skin that he was the son of gentlefolk. "Shall we keep him as our own child, wife?" Teyrnon asked her.

She took the child in her arms and laid him in the bed beside her. "Between me and heaven," said Teyrnon's wife, "from this day on we have a son indeed."

The very next day they had the boy baptised with the baptism that was then practised, and he was called Gwri Gold-hair, because the hair that was on him was yellow as gold. For three years he was reared in the court with Teyrnon, and by that time was as big as a child twice his age. By the end of his fourth year he was bargaining with the grooms of the horses to let him take the beasts to water; and it was then that Teyrnon gave him the colt which he rescued on the same night he found the boy, and the boy grew perfected in horsemanship till few in the kingdom were so skilful as he.

By this time they had heard news of Rhiannon and her penance, and one day as Teyrnon was watching the boy ride it came into his head and heart that he had never seen a lad more likely to be the son of Pwyll prince of Dyfed. He carried his mind back to the night when he found him, and realized that it was the selfsame night that Rhiannon suffered her sad loss. Grief and anger seized him together; grief that he must lose the son he loved so well, and anger for the punishment that was wrongly inflicted upon Rhiannon. As soon as he was alone with his wife he told her his thoughts, and they agreed that whatever their own grief and deprivation, they would know no happiness till they restored the boy to his rightful parents. No later than the morrow Teyrnon equipped himself, with two more horsemen, and the boy as a fourth along with them, upon the horse which Teyrnon had given him. They rode off, and it was not long before they reached Arberth. As they drew near to the court they could see a woman sitting beside the horse-block. "Shame on my beard," said Teyrnon, "if I let this wickedness last beyond today." They cantered on to the court, and soon they were abreast of her.

"Chieftain," said Rhiannon, "I pray you ride no farther. I must carry each one of you to the court, for that is my penance for slaying my son with my own hands and destroying him."

The Birth of Pryderi

"Queen and lady," said Teyrnon, "I do not think any man of mine will go upon your back."

"Go who will," vowed the boy, "I shall not go."

"No more will we," said Teyrnon.

They went on to the court, and there was great joy at their coming. Soon the joy was even greater, as Pwyll returned from a progress through Dyfed. They went to wash and then into the hall, and Pwyll made Teyrnon welcome. And before they began the carousal Teyrnon told Pwyll of his adventure with the mare and the boy, and how the boy had been taken for their own by himself and his wife, and how they had reared him and taught him horsemanship. "Send for Rhiannon," he requested Pwyll. "Her grief is greater than ours can ever be." And when she entered, "Lady," said Teyrnon, "see there your son. Lying and wrong have been practised upon you. And I believe," he added, "that there is no one in all this company who will not recognize that the boy is Pwyll's son."

"If this were so," said Rhiannon, "I should now be delivered of all my care."

"Lady," said the chieftain Pendaran Dyfed, "with that word you named your son: Pryderi son of Pwyll [Care or Thought, son of Understanding]; no other name could so become him."

"And yet," said the gracious Rhiannon, "perhaps the name he has already may suit him better."

"What name is that?" asked Pendaran Dyfed.

"Gwri Gold-hair was the name we gave him," said Teyrnon.

"No," said Pendaran Dyfed, "his name shall be Pryderi."

"It is only right," Pwyll admitted, "that his name should be taken from the word his mother spoke when she received glad tidings of him."

On this they all agreed, and Pwyll swore everlasting friendship with Teyrnon, and for Teyrnon's wife, he and Rhiannon chose gifts of beauty and price, and above all they sent her their love and gratitude. The boy was given in fosterage to Pendaran Dyfed, and soon Teyrnon returned to his own domain, and every great man who had a home elsewhere went back to it.

So the years ran by, and Pryderi, son of Pwyll, was raised with fitting care until he became the most gallant youth, and the handsomest and the best skilled in manly pursuits of any in the kingdom. And so it continued till there came an end of the life of Pwyll prince of Dyfed and he died. And then Pryderi took the kingdom, and ruled over it prosperously, and was beloved by his people and by all who came near him.

FINN AND THE YOUNG HERO'S CHILDREN

One day Finn and his men were hunting on the hill. They had killed many deer and sat in the sun out of the wind. They could see everyone and nobody could see them.

Finn saw a ship making straight for the haven beneath them. A Young Hero leaped out of her, and pulled the ship on to the green grass. Then he climbed the hill to Finn and his men.

Finn and he greeted each other, and Finn asked him where he had come from and what he wanted. He answered that he had come through the night watches and storms of the sea, because he was losing his children and only one man could help him. That man was Finn, King of the Feinne.

"I lay a spell on you," said he to Finn, "to be with me before you eat, drink or sleep."

Having said this, he left them. When he reached the ship, he pushed her, with his shoulder, into the water. Then he leaped into her, and sailed away over the horizon.

Finn said good-bye to his men, and went down to the shore. He walked along it, and saw seven men coming to meet him.

"What are you good at?" he asked the first man.

"I am a good carpenter."

"How good are you at carpentry?"

"With three strokes of my axe I can make a ship of the alder tree yonder."

"What are you good at?" he asked the second man.

"I am a good tracker."

"How good are you?"

"I can track a wild duck over the nine waves within nine days."

"What are you good at?" he asked the third man.

"I am a good gripper."

"How good are you?"

"I will not let go till my two arms part from my shoulders, or till what I hold comes with me."

"What are you good at?" he asked the fourth man.

"I am a good climber. I can climb a thread of silk to the stars, if you tie it there."

"What are you good at?" he asked the fifth man.

"I am a good thief. I can steal the heron's egg while she is watching me."

"What are you good at?" he asked the sixth man.

"I am a good listener. I can hear what people are saying at the end of the world."

"What are you good at?" he asked the seventh man.

"I am a good marksman. I could hit an egg in the sky as far away as bowstring and bow can carry the arrow."

The Carpenter went to the alder tree, and with three strokes of his axe the ship was ready. Finn ordered his seven men to push her into the water, and they went on board.

The Tracker went to the bow. Finn told him how the Young Hero had left the haven in his ship, and Finn wanted to follow him to the place where he now was. The Tracker told him to keep the ship that way or to keep her this way. They sailed a long time without seeing land, till the evening. In the gloaming they saw land ahead, and made straight for it. They leaped ashore and drew up the ship.

They walked towards a large house in the glen above the beach. As they came near it the Young Hero came to meet them.

"Dearest of all men in the world, have you come?" he said, and threw his arms about Finn's neck.

In the house, after their hunger and thirst were satisfied, the Young Hero told his story:

"Six years ago, my wife had a baby. But a large hand came down the chimney and took the child away. Three years ago, the

same thing happened. Tonight my wife is going to have another baby, and I have been told you are the only man in the world who can keep my children for me."

Finn told his men to stretch themselves on the floor, and he would keep watch. He sat beside the fire. He had an iron bar in the fire, and when his eyes began to close he pushed the bar against his palm to keep himself awake.

About midnight the baby was born, and immediately the Hand came down the chimney. Finn called the Gripper, who sprang to his feet and grasped the Hand, pulling the Giant in as far as the eyebrows. The Hand pulled the Gripper out as far as the top of his shoulders. The Gripper pulled the Hand again, and brought it in as far as the neck. The Hand pulled the Gripper, and brought him out as far as his waist. The Gripper pulled the Hand and brought it in as far as the two armpits. The Hand pulled the Gripper, and brought him out as far as the soles of his two feet. Then the Gripper gave a great pull on the Hand, and it came out of the shoulder. When it fell on the floor the pull of seven horses was in it. But the big Giant put his other hand down the chimney, and took the child away.

They were all very sorry for the loss of the child. But Finn said, "We will not give in. I and my men will go after the Hand before sunrise."

At dawn, Finn and his men launched the ship. The Tracker went to the bow, and Finn steered. The Tracker told Finn to keep her in that direction, or to keep her in this direction. They sailed far without seeing anything but the ocean. At sunset there was a black spot in the sea ahead. Finn thought it was too small for an island and too big for a bird, but he steered towards it. At dusk they reached it, and it was a rock. On top of it was a castle thatched with eelskins.

They landed on the rock, but the castle had neither window nor door, except on the roof, and the thatch was slippery.

"I'll not be long in climbing it," cried the Climber. He sprang towards the castle, and in a moment was on the roof. He looked in, took note of everything he saw, and slid down where the others were waiting.

"What did you see?" Finn asked.

125

"I saw a Giant lying on a bed, a silk covering over him, and a satin sheet under him. An infant slept in his outstretched hand. Two boys were playing shinty on the floor with sticks of gold and a silver ball. A very large deer-hound was lying beside the fire nursing her two pups."

"I don't know how we'll bring them out," said Finn.

"I'll not be long in fetching them out," said the Thief.

"Come on to my back and I'll take you to the door," said the Climber. The Thief did so, and went into the castle.

He fetched the child from the Giant's hand, the two boys who were playing, the silk covering from over the Giant, and the satin sheet from under him. Then he fetched the sticks of gold and the silver ball, and the two pups from their mother. There was nothing else of value, so he left the Giant sleeping and came out.

They put everything into the ship and sailed away. Soon after that the Listener stood up.

"I hear him," he said.

"What do you hear?" said Finn.

"He has just wakened," said the Listener, "and missed everything we stole. He is very angry. He's sending the deer-hound. He's telling her that if she won't go he'll go himself. It's the hound that's coming."

Soon behind them they saw the hound coming. She was swimming so fast, red sparks were coming from her. They were afraid.

"Throw out one of the pups," said Finn. "Maybe when she sees the pup drowning, she'll go back with it." They threw out the pup, and she went back with it.

Soon after the Listener stood up, trembling.

"I hear him," he said.

"What do you hear now?" asked Finn.

"He's sending the hound again. But as she won't go, he's coming himself."

After they heard this, their eyes were always behind them. At last they saw him coming, and the ocean rose no farther than his thighs. They were terribly afraid, and didn't know what to do. But Finn thought of his wisdom tooth, and put his finger under it. He learned that the Giant was immortal, except for a mole on his palm.

"If I catch one glimpse of it, I'll have him," said the Marksman.

The Giant waded through the sea to the side of the ship. He put up his hand to seize the top of the mast, to sink the ship. But when his hand was up, the Marksman saw the mole and let fly an arrow which hit the spot, and the Giant fell dead into the sea.

They turned about, and sailed back to the castle. The Thief again stole the pup, and they took it along with the one they had. They returned to the Young Hero. In the haven they leaped ashore, and pulled the ship on to dry land.

Then Finn went to the Young Hero's house, taking with him the Young Hero's family and everything he and his men had taken out of the Giant's castle.

The Young Hero met him, and when he saw his children he kneeled before Finn.

"What reward do you want?" he said.

"I ask for nothing but my choice of the two pups we took from the castle."

This pup was Bran, and his brother that the Young Hero got, was the Grey Dog.

The Young Hero took Finn and his men into his house, and made a merry feast which lasted for a year and a day, and if the last day was not the best, it was not the worst.

GARETH AND LINETTE

O nce King Arthur went to keep the feast of Whitsuntide in a castle close by the border of Wales. Now, he had a custom that on Whitsunday he would never sit down to meat until he had seen some wonder or heard of some marvellous adventure.

On this day as he waited to begin the feasting, a youth followed by a dwarf rode into the courtyard, dismounted, and came into the hall. He was a very tall and broad young man, with a happy face and hands that were large and strong; and as he strode up the hall all eyes watched him with approval.

"You are welcome, stranger," said Arthur. "Sit down and eat with us."

But the youth replied, "Greetings, to you, my lord king, and to your fellowship. I have come here this day to ask three favours. The first I shall ask now, if you will permit me, and the other two a year from today."

Arthur smiled. "Ask what you will. I do not think that I shall refuse you."

"I ask only," said the youth, "that you will give me meat and drink and a place in your household until a year is passed and I may ask for two last boons."

"It is a poor request," said Arthur. "I should be glad to give you more than that."

"It is all I ask," said the youth.

"Then you shall have your fill of meat and drink for twelve months," said Arthur. "God forbid that I should refuse his keep to any man. But tell me now your name."

"Forgive me, my lord king," replied the youth, "but that I cannot tell you yet."

Arthur smiled again. "Let it be as you wish." Then turning to Sir Kay the Seneschal he said, "Let this young man have of our best for a year, and though we do not know his name, let him be treated as if he were the son of a nobleman, and see that he lacks nothing."

But Kay was indignant that Arthur was prepared to spare good food and drink for one who might not merit it. "The son of a nobleman!" he exclaimed. "He is more likely the son of a peasant. The son of a nobleman would have asked you for a horse and armour, not for a twelvemonth's food. And as for his having no name, I can find him a name easily enough." He glanced with scorn at the youth's hands, which were so large that they seemed almost clumsy. "I shall call him Beaumains, Fair-hands, and unless he is as lazy as he is large, I shall find him work enough in the kitchen, where he may earn his keep."

"Do not be over hard in my interests, Kay," said Arthur, who knew well his foster-brother's cross-grained loyalty and loved him for it.

But the stranger smiled. "I will do whatever work you demand of me, Sir Kay."

Yet Sir Lancelot, hearing Kay's words, did not smile. "Shame on you, Kay," he called from where he sat, "to mock at a lad who has done you no harm, and who, I dare say, will one day prove himself worthy of our fellowship."

And though he said nothing, Sir Gawaine, King Arthur's nephew, stared closely at the youth, wondering why, though he had seen the tall stranger for the first time not above a few moments before, he should instantly have felt that he knew him.

"What he has asked for, I have offered him," said Kay. "Now let him find himself a place to sit and eat, for we have seen a wonder sufficient to satisfy our lord the king this Whitsunday: a youth, tall and strong enough, with his wits and his health, who has no wish for anything in life but food and drink."

So Beaumains, as they called him from that day, went and sat below the salt, among the serving-lads, without another word. And the dwarf who had accompanied him mounted his master's horse and left the castle, answering the questions of none.

But when the feasting was over, Gawaine went to the youth, wondering why he did so, and offered to take him as his squire. Beaumains turned his head away and would not look him in the face. "I thank you for your kindness, Sir Gawaine," he said, "but I will do as Sir Kay has bidden me, for in all things he must be my master."

"It shall be as you wish it," said Gawaine.

Then Sir Lancelot, with his usual courtesy and gentleness, came and spoke to Beaumains, offering him food and wine and lodging and good company; and this time Beaumains did not turn away, but looked Lancelot in the face and smiled and said, "I thank you for your kindness, Sir Lancelot, but I will do as Sir Kay has bidden me, for in all things he must be my master."

"It shall be as you wish it," said Lancelot. "But if ever at any time you would ask a service of me, it shall willingly be rendered."

"One day," replied Beaumains, "I hope to ask a service of you, Sir Lancelot."

So for twelve months Beaumains worked in the kitchen; turning the meat on the spits, baking the bread, and fetching pails of water from the well, and never a word did he say as to his name or whence he had come, and never once did he grumble at his lot, but was always cheerful and well mannered. And in the summer evenings, when the kitchen lads would gather in the courtyard after their day's work was over, to try themselves with feats of strength and wrestling, Beaumains was always proved the strongest of them. And always when there were jousting and tournaments, so long as his work did not forbid it, Beaumains would be there, among the servants, looking on eagerly, a great light of longing shining in his eyes.

When a year had passed and Whitsunday came round once more, again King Arthur would not sit down to the feasting until some wonder or adventure came to him; and while he waited a richly dressed damsel rode up to the castle and asked to speak with him.

"I would have the help of one of your boldest knights, lord king," she said, "for the sake of my lady who is besieged in her castle by the evil Red Knight of the Red Plain, whose name is Sir Ironside."

"I have heard of this Red Knight," said Gawaine. "He is indeed an evil knight, and with the strength of seven men."

"Willingly shall I and my knights give you our help, damsel," said Arthur, "if you will tell us the name of your lady and where she dwells."

"That I may not do," replied the damsel.

"It is asking too much of one of my knights," said Arthur gently, "that he should ride with you to serve an unknown lady in lands you will not name."

"I did not think that King Arthur would refuse me my request," said the damsel. "But now I see that I must ask elsewhere." And she gathered up the train of her gown and made to leave the hall.

But Beaumains stepped forward from among the servants and knelt before Arthur. "My lord king," he said, "I have been in your service for a year, may I now ask of you the last two favours?"

"Ask what you will," said Arthur.

"Then, my lord king, let me undertake this adventure for the unknown lady who is assailed by the Red Knight, and also grant that when I shall ask it, I may receive knighthood at the hands of that one of your knights whom I most respect."

Arthur was glad that the unknown youth showed a desire for

adventure and for knighthood, and he answered, "It shall be as you wish."

But the damsel was indignant and cried out, "Is this the far-famed courtesy of King Arthur, that he offers me no more than a kitchen-lad to serve my lady?" And with her head held high she swept from the hall, mounted her horse, and rode away.

Beaumains went out into the courtyard, and even as he stood there, the same dwarf who had accompanied him to the court twelve months before came through the gates, leading a fine horse and bearing armour and a sword. "I have returned as you bade me, master," he said, and helped Beaumains arm himself. Then Beaumains, having neither shield or lance, mounted the horse and rode after the damsel, with the dwarf running at the horse's side.

"This is a fine thing," grumbled Sir Kay, "that my kitchen-lad arms himself like a knight and the son of a lord and rides off on an adventure. Let us see how he acquits himself when a true knight opposes him." And with that he called for his own horse and his armour and rode off after Beaumains, in spite of the protests of Lancelot and Gawaine, who wished no ill to come to the youth.

Just as Beaumains overtook the damsel, Sir Kay caught up with him and called out to him to wait. 'I am going to fight the Red Knight for the sake of this damsel's lady, and I may not wait," said Beaumains quietly.

"You are impertinent," said Kay. "Do you not know who I am?"

Beaumains smiled a little. "I know you well. You are the most ungentle knight in all King Arthur's court."

Kay was angry and rode straight at Beaumains, for all that the youth had neither lance nor shield; but Beaumains thrust Kay's lance aside with his sword and struck him such a blow that Sir Kay fell from his horse and lay stunned upon the ground. Then Beaumains bade his dwarf give him Kay's shield and lance, and ordered him to ride upon Kay's horse since he had none of his own.

But as Beaumains was about to ride on again after the damsel, he caught sight of Lancelot who had ridden after Kay and seen all that had happened. "Sir Lancelot," he called, "will you joust with me?"

"Willingly," said Lancelot. They rode at each other and at the first blow Lancelot unhorsed Beaumains, and dismounting drew his sword and fought with him on foot. And Lancelot was glad to find how strong and quick young Beaumains was, that even he, who was the best of knights in Britain, was well matched by him, and he laughed and cried out, "Come, Beaumains, we have no quarrel so great that we should fight all day for it."

"I did but wish to prove my worth to you," said Beaumains, lowering his sword.

"And you have proved it well," said Lancelot.

Beaumains took off his helmet. "Shall I soon be worthy of knighthood?" he asked eagerly.

"You are worthy of knighthood at this moment," said Lancelot.

Beaumains' face was alight with joy. "Then before I go on my first adventure, will you make me a knight? For of all in Arthur's court there is no one by whom I would rather be knighted than by you, who have shown me so much kindness and are the best knight in all the land."

"It is a thing which I shall do most willingly," said Lancelot, "but first you must tell me your name."

"I am Gareth of Orkney, brother to Gawaine and nephew of the king. But I beg you will tell no one of it until I am returned from this adventure."

"I had no doubt that you were of noble birth," said Lancelot, "for all that you asked so little of the king."

So Gareth, who had been called Beaumains, knelt down on the grass and Lancelot took up his sword and knighted him. Then he said, "Now ride on your adventure, and may you be successful, and I will see Kay safely home."

So Gareth rode on quickly, followed by his dwarf, and after a time he caught up with the damsel who had ridden on as soon as she had seen Sir Kay unhorsed. She greeted Gareth with scorn. "I hoped that I would see no more of you, you kitchen-lad. Must you still plague me with your company? Why do you follow me? For you will never dare to face the Red Knight."

"I can but try," said Gareth quietly. And for a time they rode on in silence, the damsel with her head held high and Gareth a little way behind.

Gareth and Linette

Then suddenly, towards evening, as they journeyed through a wood, a man came running towards them and clutched hold of the bridle of Gareth's horse. "I beg you, help my master," he cried. "For he has been attacked by robbers and I fear they will kill him."

"Take me to him," said Gareth. The man led him a little way off the path to where his master lay bound, with six robbers dividing his arms and his gold between them. When they saw Gareth approaching, they leapt to their feet and made to run away, but with three strokes Gareth killed three of them and then pursued the others until all six were slain.

The knight whom he had rescued made much of Gareth, and since it was close on nightfall, offered him the hospitality of his near-by castle until the morning.

"I follow this damsel on an adventure," said Gareth. "If it is pleasing to her to ride on all through the night, then so must I. But if she will accept your offer, then I will follow her to your castle."

And because it was growing dark and she was weary, the damsel rode with the knight to his castle, talking most courteously to him, but ever bearing herself as though Gareth were not there.

In his castle the knight called for meat and wine and set the damsel at his high table and bade her eat. But when he would have called Gareth to the place beside her, she cried out, "Shame on you for a discourteous host, who would expect a noblewoman to eat in the company of a kitchen-lad."

The knight was ashamed that she should speak thus of one who had done him so great a service, and he ordered his servants to set a table for Gareth at the other side of the hall, and went himself and ate apart with him, while the damsel supped alone in angry silence.

In the morning Gareth and the damsel took leave of their host and rode on. After a time they reached a wide river, and there was in sight only one place where it was shallow enough to be forded, but on the farther side the ford was guarded by two knights who called out that none might cross the river unless he fought with them.

"You had best ride home, scullion," taunted the damsel.

"Indeed I shall not," said Gareth, and he rode on into the river.

One of the knights rode forward, and in the very midst of the river they met and fought, and the strange knight was thrown from his horse into the water, and so drowned. On the farther bank Gareth fought with the second knight and slew him with a mighty stroke. Then he bade the damsel cross in safety.

All the way across she railed at him, "That I should live to see the day when two fine knights should perish at the hands of a greasy kitchen-lad! Yet you need not flatter yourself that you have fought manfully today, for I saw the horse of the first knight slip and throw him, and so was he drowned by misadventure. And as for the second, you struck him from behind, false and cowardly as you are."

But to all her unjust words Gareth gave no answer save, "I have come to serve and win your lady, and I shall do it or die."

"You will not die, never fear," scoffed the damsel, "for at the first sight of the Red Knight you will turn and fly."

A little way beyond the river, beneath a gnarled old hawthorn tree, stood a great black horse with a knight in black armour upon its back, bearing a black shield.

"It is the Black Knight," said the damsel. "He is famed for his strength. Turn and make for home, scullion, while there is yet time."

"I thank you for your care of me, lady," said Gareth, "but I will allow not even you to make me a coward."

The Black Knight recognized the damsel and called out to her, "Greetings, Lady Linette. Is this the champion from King Arthur's court whom you went to fetch?"

"Indeed it is not," replied the damsel indignantly. "It is no more than a kitchen-lad who has followed me against my will. I shall be much in your debt if you will rid me of his company."

"It would be a lasting shame to me that I should fight with a kitchen-lad," said the Black Knight. "But his horse and his armour I will take from him, and he may return to his kitchen on foot."

"My horse and my armour are mine," said Gareth, "and I can well defend them."

And they rode against each other, while Linette and the dwarf looked on. The Black Knight's lance broke, so that he and Gareth drew their swords and fought on foot, and at last Gareth killed him. And because Kay's shield which he carried had been battered in the fight, he took with him the black shield that had belonged to the Black Knight, and rode upon the Black Knight's horse, for it was fresher than his own.

And ever Linette upbraided him for a cowardly kitchen-lad who slew good knights by mischance, and bade him begone from her.

"Lady," said Gareth, "you might as well leave your railing, for I will follow you as long as I may. And as for your counselling me to flee whenever danger shows, it seems to me that it would have been better had you saved your counsel for those I fought against." But his words only made her more angry.

Then suddenly they saw approaching them a knight in green armour, with a green shield, and green harness on his horse; and seeing the shield which Gareth carried, this knight called out, "Are you my brother, the Black Knight?"

But before Gareth could reply, Linette cried, "It is not the Black Knight. It is no more than a common scullion who has killed your brother and carries his shield."

Then the Green Knight was angry and bade Gareth defend himself, calling him a murderer. "I slew your brother in fair fight," said Gareth. And he fought with the Green Knight while Linette stood by and rallied his opponent, reminding him of the shame it would be to a knight to be worsted by a kitchen-lad. But at last Gareth overcame the Green Knight, who yielded to him and begged his mercy.

"Your life is lost," said Gareth, "unless this damsel asks for it."

"Do you think that I would ask a favour of a scullion?" cried Linette.

"Then must this brave knight die," said Gareth, "and all for want of a word from you."

"Lady, have pity on me and speak for me," pleaded the Green Knight.

Yet Linette would not hear him and only said, "I will ask no favours of a greasy kitchen-lad."

Gareth took off the Green Knight's helmet and made as though he would cut off his head, and Linette pitied the Green Knight and cried out, though reluctantly, "Release him, scullion, or you will repent it!"

Gareth smiled. "It is a pleasure to do you a favour, lady." And Linette stamped her little foot and turned away.

That night they lodged at the Green Knight's manor which was close by. And once again Linette would not sit to eat with Gareth, though the Green Knight rebuked her for it; so Gareth ate alone at a little table.

The next day Gareth and Linette set out again, and after a short ride they reached a tall white tower. As they passed by this tower a knight in crimson armour, carrying a crimson shield, rode forth to them, calling out to Gareth, "Is it you, my brother the Black Knight?"

And Linette replied immediately, "It is not your brother. It is no more than a kitchen-lad who has slain the Black Knight and carries his shield."

When the Crimson Knight heard that his brother was dead, he rode in anger at Gareth and a great combat they had there, while Linette watched them. And at last the Crimson Knight yielded to Gareth and pleaded for his life; and Gareth answered, "I will spare you only if this damsel will speak for you." And he flourished his sword as though he would have cut off the Crimson Knight's head.

Linette was angry, but she could not see a brave knight die for want of a word from her, so grudgingly she said, "Release him, wretched kitchen-lad, or it will be the worse for you."

Gareth smiled. "It is a pleasure, lady, to do you a favour."

Gareth and Linette rode on together, followed by the dwarf, and all the way she never ceased to taunt him and upbraid him, though he answered her no word in reply. At last they came to a field before a castle where there were many pavilions set up as for a jousting, and they were all blue with blue pennons flying in the breeze. And the moment that she saw them Linette grew silent and thoughtful.

As they rode by, a knight spied them from his pavilion, armed himself and rode forth to meet them; and he was all in blue armour, carrying a blue shield, and the harness of his charger was blue.

Gareth and Linette

Linette reined in her horse and said to Gareth, "That is the Blue Knight coming towards us, and he is stronger by far than his brothers. Fly while there is yet time."

"I have fought with the others, I shall fight with him," replied Gareth.

But Linette spoke again, and this time her voice was no longer scornful and cold, and she turned away as though she were ashamed. "Even though you are a serving-lad, you have proved yourself brave. Well have you fought and gently have you received my harsh words. I would not see you shamed or slain through engaging with one too strong for you."

"Now that you have spoken kindly of me, I have all the more reason for courage. Fear not for me, lady." And Gareth rode forward to meet the Blue Knight and fought long with him, until at last the Blue Knight was overcome and pleaded for his life. And this time Linette spoke at once. "Give him his life, Beaumains, for he is a noble knight."

Gareth and Linette were welcomed at the Blue Knight's pavilion, and there they ate together in good company and fellowship, and there they passed the night. And in the morning, when they would have set out again, Linette begged Gareth that he would agree to be knighted by the Blue Knight. "For," she said, "today we shall reach the castle of my lady, who is my sister, the Lady Lionesse, and there you will meet with the Red Knight of the Red Plain, and it is only right that one who has proved himself worthy should be made a knight before undertaking a fearful task."

But Gareth told her how he had been knighted by Sir Lancelot after he had fought with Sir Kay, and he told her that he was Gareth of Orkney and nephew to King Arthur, and she rejoiced that he was after all of noble birth and not a serving-lad, and asked for his forgiveness for her scorn. "Lady," he replied, "I have forgotten all you said to me."

So they went on towards her sister's castle, and before it they saw the pavilions of the Red Knight and his men, and near by a tree with a horn hanging from a branch. "Whoever would challenge the Red Knight must blow on that horn," said Linette.

Gareth set the horn to his lips and blew a mighty blast, and the evil Red Knight, Sir Ironside, came forth from his pavilion and armed himself all in red; and mounted upon a flame-coloured horse, he awaited Gareth on a level stretch of ground right below the castle walls.

"See," said Linette, "where my sister looks down upon you from that window. Now at last may she be delivered from her enemy."

And Gareth looked up and beheld the most beautiful lady he had ever seen, and swore to himself to save her and win her or die, and he galloped forward to meet the Red Knight. They came together with such force that each unhorsed the other, but as quickly as they might they rose to their feet and drew their swords. And so they fought for more than half a day. The Red Knight was a hardy fighter, and much experienced in battle, so that Gareth was all but overcome. Then he looked up at the window where the Lady Lionesse watched, and he took courage and made one final effort and struck the Red Knight upon the helm so that he was stunned and dropped his sword. Gareth unlaced his helm to cut off his head, and the Red Knight yielded and asked mercy.

"I will spare you only if you will promise to leave off your evil ways," said Gareth. And the Red Knight gave his word to live peaceably from that day, and with all his men he departed to his own lands, and the Lady Lionesse was free.

Later, when Gareth was healed of his wounds, he entered the castle and met the Lady Lionesse, and she seemed to him even more beautiful than when he had first seen her at the window. And he seemed to her the finest and the bravest knight in all the world. He took her back to King Arthur's court with him, and there they were married. And a little time later, his brother Gaheris married the Lady Linette.

Arthur had made much of Gareth when he knew that he was his nephew, and Gawaine and Gaheris had greeted him joyfully as their younger brother whom they had not seen since he was a child. But of all knights Gareth loved best Sir Lancelot, who was ever a good friend to him.

And in time the Red Knight of the Red Plain, whose name was Sir Ironside, having thought long on the courtesy and courage of Gareth, came to Arthur's court and offered his services to the king. He proved himself as good as he had once been wicked, and was at last admitted to the fellowship of the Round Table.

HOW CORMAC MAC ART GOT HIS BRANCH

On a day long ago, when time was still in its early freshness, Cormac Mac Art, the arch-king of Erin, was walking on the ridge of Liath known as Liathdrum; his figure was outlined against the blue of the sky, and the wind tossed the folds of his dark, blue cloak, so that it bellied out like the outspread sails of a ship, and at his side walked his lean grey wolfhound Cion.

And so it was that he saw a tall, fair-seeming youth on the green near the Dun, clasping in his right hand a glittering fairy branch, and clustered upon it were nine apples of a wondrous red-gold colour.

And this branch had many magical virtues, and in this manner: that if any man wounded in combat, or woman in sickness, or weary babe had the branch shaken over them, they were instantly lulled into a sweet sleep by reason of the silver music made by the apples. Another of its properties was that no one living could remember aught of woe, or hunger, or soul-sickness, nor any other evil that might have befallen them once they heard the shaking of that branch.

Then Cormac said to the youth, "Is the branch belonging to you?"

And the youth made answer, "It is indeed mine own."

And Cormac was filled with longing to have the branch, and he asked, "Would you sell it to me?"

And the youth replied, "I would sell it if I might name the price."

Then Cormac said eagerly, "Name it."

Whereupon the youth answered, "I would have thy wife, thy son, and thy daughter."

"If I may have the branch you may take them all," said Cormac.

After that the youth puts the branch into Cormac's hand, and Cormac bears it to his house, and shows it to Ailbe his wife, and to Eithne his son, and to Caire his daughter.

"That is a strange, fair treasure you have there," says his wife.

"A treasure it is, but I gave a fair price for it," answers Cormac.

"And what was the offer or exchange you made for it?" says Ailbe.

"I gave in exchange Caire, Eithne and yourself, O Ailbe," says Cormac.

"Now here is a foolish joke," says Ailbe, "for we know well that there is no treasure in the whole world that you would take in our place."

"Nevertheless," answers Cormac, "I swear to you that I have given you in exchange for this branch."

Then grief and shame overcame all three, and they began to look harshly at Cormac—and Eithne his son said to him:

"It is too hard a bargain for us three, nor will we agree to it for any branch in the world."

But when Cormac saw the heaviness that was upon them, he lifted the branch, and shook it gently between them; and when they heard the soft, lilting music of the apples they had no further thought of the evil that had befallen them, but turning away from Cormac, they hastened forth to meet the youth.

Then Cormac also went out, and he said to the youth:

"Here is the price you require for this branch, nor do I grudge it, though my house will be empty in the coming days."

"You have fulfilled your promise without faltering," said the youth, "and I give you a blessing for the sake of your truth, and may you have many victories."

And with that, he and his company vanished out of sight. And when this news was first heard throughout Erin, loud cries of mourning and the sound of weeping rose into the heavens, and in Liathdrum louder than elsewhere. But Cormac took the fairy branch, and he went to and fro among the people, shaking the branch in their hearing; and all heaviness of heart and distress was forgotten—and for that time there was peace and contentment.

Soon then a year had gone by—and suddenly Cormac remembered the day on which his wife, and his son, and his daughter had been taken from him, and a heaviness of spirit fell upon him in that moment (for the magic branch was not at his side); and he said to himself:

"I will go out and follow after them on the way I saw them take, until I come to the place where they now dwell."

So Cormac set forth on his long journey; and while he was seeking for the path taken by the youth of the magic branch, a dark, strange mist rose up all around him — and groping slowly through its enshrouding folds, he came on a great and marvellous plain.

And thus it was on the plain: a great host of horsemen, many hundreds in number were there, and the work they were occupied with was this — they were building a cover of feathers over a house, and the feathers were those of strange birds from far-off lands, and were of rich and varied hues, scarlets, and blues, and greens, and gold shining through the mist. But at no time had the horsemen enough feathers to cover more than half the house, so that they were obliged to leave their toil, and go to seek for more feathers. And when they returned, they found that all those feathers which they had closed together with such care and labour had vanished.

Now Cormac stood there a long time, wondering why they sought to cover-in the house thus; and seeing them return from their travels again and again only to find their work undone, he said:

"I will not stay here to watch them, for I can see that they will be toiling until the end of the world and nothing done." So he went on his way.

Still the great wondrous plain stretched out before him, now half hidden by the mist, now revealed in flashes of bright colour as if shafts of sunlight struck down upon it. And when Cormac had gone some distance, and had begun to weary of the solitude, he saw a strange, foreign-seeming youth walking in front of him, and this is what he was doing: he sought about until he came upon a great tree, and stooping, pulled it lightly out of the ground, and broke it in two halves betwixt the top and the bottom; and then he would make a huge, heaped fire of the tree, so that the flames leapt up to meet the clouds overhead. And when the fire was lit, he would go and seek another tree, and bring it to that place. But always he found that the fire had burnt away to a pile of ashes, and nothing remained save wisps and shreds on the ground, so that each time he was forced to start another fire. And this he continued to do.

So for a great space Cormac stood there, and watched the youth at his labours, and pitied his plight. But at last he said to himself:

"I will go further, for were I to watch him until the world ended he would still be thus."

After this, Cormac walked for many leagues, and time had no longer any meaning, so that day and night were one; and whether he had journeyed for a week or a year he knew not. But suddenly he saw that he was near to the border of the plain, and there, rising up before him were three immense wells, and sticking up out of each well was a human head.

Then Cormac drew near to the first well, and he perceived that the head had a stream of water flowing into one side of its mouth, and two streams coming fast out of the other side. So after he had gazed long at this strange sight Cormac went to the second well; and there the head had one stream flowing into its mouth, and one flowing out. Then Cormac came to the third well; and there he saw that the head had three broad streams flowing into its mouth, but only one coming out. Now a deep cloud of wonderment filled Cormac's mind, and we do not know how long he stood there thinking on the matter; but at last he drew nearer to the heads, and said to them:

"Surely this is a great marvel; but I will not stay here any longer with no man to tell me your histories. Yet I think I might find some good sense in this mystery could I but understand it."

So the King of Erin went on his way, and soon enough he saw in front of him a very great field, and a house in the middle of it. And he drew near, and entered into the house, and greeted those who were within; and when his eyes became accustomed to the dimness, he saw there a very tall couple, wearing clothes of many varied hues. And they made answer to his greeting, and bade him stay with them, "for," said they, "whomsoever you are, it is now no time for you to be travelling on foot." Hereupon Cormac, son of Art, sits down, and right glad was he to find hospitality for that night.

Now when he was seated, the young man of the house also sat him down by the fire, but the woman turned to him and said:

"Rise you, O man of the house, for there is a handsome, comely wanderer by us, and how know you but that he may be some honourable noble of the men of the world? And if you have one kind of food or meat of your plenty that is better than another, bring it here to me."

On hearing these words the young man arose, and went out of the house; and presently he came back to them thus — with a huge wild boar carried on his back, and a log in his right hand, and he cast them both down on the floor and said:

"There ye have meat and fire — cook it for yourselves."

"And how shall we do that same?" asks Cormac.

"I will teach you that," answers the young man; "you must split this great log and make four pieces of it and cut the pig into four quarters; and let you put one quarter on top of a quarter of the log, and tell a true story, and that quarter will be cooked when the tale is done."

"Tell the first story yourself," says Cormac, "for the two should rightly tell a story for the one and he a guest in the house."

"You speak rightly," says the young man, "and I think it likely that you have the manners of a prince, so I will tell you a tale to begin with, and here it is. That swine there," he went on, "I have but seven of them, and I could feed the world with them; for when you kill one, you have but to take all the bones, and put them back in the sty again, and it will be found alive on the morrow."

As he stopped speaking they all turned to look at the quarter of the pig on top of the log — and that story was true, for it was cooked.

"Tell you a story now, O woman of the house," said the young man.

"I will tell it," quoth she, "and let you put a quarter of the pig down, with a quarter of the log under it." So it was done.

"Well then," said she, "I have seven white cows, and they fill seven kieves with their milk each day, and I give you my word that they would give enough milk as would satisfy the men of the whole world, and they out there on the plain drinking it."

And that story was true, and the quarter of the boar was cooked.

Then Cormac spoke, and he said:

"If your stories be true, it is certain that you are Manannan, ruler of the sea, and the woman of the house is your wife; for no one upon the back of the earth has possession of such treasures but only Manannan Mac Lir. And was it not to Tir Tairrngire he went seeking the woman, and she bringing the seven cows with her; and a year and a day it took him to learn the powers of their milking."

"Wisely have you spoken, O wanderer," said the man of the house, "and now we are waiting to hear your story that you may win your quarter of the pig."

"That will I do," said Cormac, "and do you lay a quarter in the cauldron, and a quarter of the log under it, and my tale will be a true one." So it was done. Then Cormac began his story, and he said:

"Now I can tell you that a year ago it was this day that my wife, my son, and my daughter were borne away from me—and so I am seeking out the place where they lodge."

"And who took them from you?" asked the young man.

"Well then," said Cormac, "a fair-seeming youth came to me, holding in his right hand a fairy branch, and on it hung apples possessed of magical virtues. And a great desire seized upon me to own that branch, so that I was willing to grant him what award he should require of me, and I gave him my word to fulfil his demand. And the price he asked of me was my wife, my son, and my daughter, and they are named Ailbe, Eithne, and Caire."

"If these words be truth," said the man of the house, "you are indeed Cormac, son of Art, son of Conn of the Hundred Battles."

"That am I," said Cormac, "and it is in search of my dear ones that you see me now."

And that story was true for the pig was cooked.

"Eat your meat now," said the young man.

But Cormac answered, "I have never eaten food with only two people in my company."

"Would you eat it with three others, O Cormac?" asked the young man.

"If they were dear to me I would eat," said Cormac.

Then the young man rose, and he opened a door which was

near to him, and he went through it—and after a time he returned, bringing those three of whom Cormac had spoken. And courage and exultation filled the heart of Cormac. And when the greetings were done, Manannan came to Cormac in his proper form, clothed in his silver cloak of light, and with the brightness of morning in his face, and said thus:

"It was I who bore these three away from you, O Cormac, so let you be easy now and eat your food."

"I will do that," said Cormac, "if you will tell me the meaning of the three wonders I have seen this day."

"You shall learn of them," answered Manannan, "and it was myself that caused the mist to rise round you, that you might be guided to see them.

"The horsemen that appeared before you, covering the house with feathers, which disappeared as they were seeking more feathers for the rest of it; let you compare them to poets, and to those people who go forth to seek a fortune; for when they go out, all that they leave behind in their houses is spent, and so they go on seeking for ever.

"The youth that you saw kindling a fire to burn the tree which he had broken into pieces, and who found it consumed by the fire when he returned with another tree, let you think of him as representing those who serve food while other men eat of it; but while they themselves get it ready, others have all the profit of it.

"The wells you saw with a head in each one, are to be compared with the three sorts of men who are in the world, and these are they. The first one is the man who gives away the goods of this world as he receives them; and that head which you saw with one stream flowing into its mouth and two flowing out, has the meaning of that man who gives more than he gets of this world's goods; and that head which had three streams flowing into its mouth, but only one coming out, that is the man who gets much, but gives little—and he is the worst of the three. And now eat your meal, O Cormac," said Manannan.

So after that, Cormac, Ailbe, Eithne, and Caire sat down in that house, and a fine white cloth was spread before them. And Manannan said to Cormac:

"That is a precious thing spread before you, O Cormac, for

there is no food, however delicate and rare that shall be demanded of it, but you shall receive it as you speak the words."

"That is indeed a wonder," said Cormac.

Then Manannan put his hand to his girdle, and brought forth a goblet, encrusted with jewels, which sent out fiery flashes of light as he moved, and he set it on the palm of his hand.

"It is certain that this cup possesses many virtues," said he, "and among them is this, that when a false story is told before it, the cup will fall into four pieces; but when a true tale is related, it will come together in one piece."

"Let you prove that same," said Cormac.

"I will do so," said Manannan. "This woman, your wife, whom I took from you. She has taken another husband since she has dwelt here."

And instantly the cup fell in four pieces on to the floor.

"That is a false tale," said the wife of Manannan, "for she has seen no man save my husband since she was taken from you."

And that story was true, for the goblet was joined together again in that moment.

"These are indeed precious and wondrous things that you have, O Manannan," said Cormac.

"It would be good that you should be having them," said Manannan, "therefore shall all three be yours, namely the branch, the table-cloth, and the goblet; and I give them to you with my blessing in consideration for the walk and the journey that you have had this day. And eat your meal now, for were there a host in this place you would find no grudging here. And I ask your forgiveness for the magic I worked upon you that you might eat with me this night."

After that Cormac eats his meal, and so good it was that never had he or his companions eaten so well before. For there was no meat or delicacy that they thought on, but it was there on the cloth before them, nor any drinks but they got them in the cup, and many were the healths drunk, and the thanks given to Manannan.

Howbeit, when the feast was over, beds were prepared for them, and they sank into a deep, sweet, restful slumber. And when they woke on the morrow, where should they find themselves but in Liathdrum, with the table-cloth, the branch, and the cup.

Thus far then the seeking of Cormac and how he got his branch.

JOSEPH AND HIS BRETHREN

This is a story that ends in Egypt, but it does not begin there. It begins more than a hundred years before Moses was found in the bulrushes: and it began with an old oak tree at Hebron in Palestine and in a big black tent.

It was an old tent, for first of all Abraham had lived there, and then his son Isaac, and now it belonged to Isaac's son Jacob. Jacob had been in foreign parts nearly all his life, but when he was old he came back to the old oak and the old tent, and settled down. But there was a crowd of little tents round it now, for he had twelve sons, and many herds of cows and sheep and goats. But at the time this story begins it was very quiet in the big black tent, for ten of the older sons were away, and the only two at home were Joseph and a very little one called Benjamin. Joseph was the son that his father liked best, except of course for Benjamin: but then everyone loved Benjamin, he was so fat and so small, tumbling about like a puppy. Even the big brothers, who were a very rough lot, liked Benjamin. But they hated Joseph: he was their step-

149

brother, and his father's favourite, and they jeered at him for his
good manners and his pride and his queer, dreamy ways; they
were jealous of him. They thought he was a conceited cub, and it
made things worse when their father gave him a coat that was all
bright colours. They were always teasing him and making fun of
him, especially on account of one of his dreams which seemed to
mean that he would be set in authority over them. Joseph was not
sorry when the whole ten cleared off early one morning with
droves and droves of sheep to graze them on the green fields of
Shechem, for the grass round Hebron was now all trampled and
bare. There was a mountain between called Gerizim, rocky and
barren, but on the other side of it the grass was green and deep.

So the days went by, and the old man began to wonder how
the boys were, for he had a heart for them all. So he called Joseph
and told him he wanted him to go and find his brothers: he need
not stay, just see how they all were, and if the sheep were getting
fat, and bring word home. So Joseph put some dates and cheese
and bread in his wallet and said good-bye and started off.

It was a long way to Shechem. Joseph slept under a tree one
night and the next night in a cave, but at last he saw the steep
rocks of Gerizim in front of him, and knew the green fields of
Shechem would be on the other side.

When he had got to the ridge of the hill, he stopped and looked.
He could see the fields for miles, but they were dark and quiet,
never a glimmer of fire or a bleat from a sheep, just the quiet of
the hills and the coming of night. He couldn't believe it: he hurried down the mountain-side, and tramped up and down, shouting
and whistling, and just as he had given up hope a man came to
him over the darkening fields.

"What have you lost?" said he.

"I am looking for my brothers," said Joseph. "They were grazing their sheep. Please, did you see them anywhere?"

"They went away out of this," said the man, "but I heard them
say they were going on to Dothan."

Joseph's face fell. "Is it far?" said he. "It is the better part of
ten miles," said the man. "But let you come home with me and
have bite and sup, and I'll put you on the road in the morning."

And with that he took Joseph home to his tent, and brought

him a bowl of milk, but before Joseph had finished it he was fast asleep. And next morning he started off early, before the dew was dry on the grass, with a handful of dates in his pocket, and the kind man told him the way and said with any luck he would be there by dinner time.

Joseph's big brothers had been very busy all morning, but now they were lying on the grass and waiting till dinner was ready. And suddenly one of them said, "What's that?" And they all got up and looked, and away, away on the hot white road they saw a little speck moving. It was such a lonely country that they couldn't think who it would be, and they watched while the speck drew nearer, and then the one with the sharpest eyes saw that it was someone in a bright-coloured coat, and said with his sneering laugh, "Here's the dreamer coming." They stood and watched him trudging up the road, very far away, and you would think they might have been sorry for the young brother tramping so far to find them all by himself. But the old jealousy leaped up in them, like the flames when you put the poker into the fire, and it burned all the pity out of them. They thought of all the times their father had thrashed them when he found them hurting him, and all the ways he had that they hated, and they said, "Now's our chance to pay him out. We'll kill him, and throw him into a pit, and tell our father a lion must have killed him somewhere on the road. And we'll see what becomes of his dreams."

Now Reuben had always a liking for Joseph, but he was not brave enough to stand up against all the rest. So he said, "Don't kill him. Throw him into that old pit there, and leave him, but don't hurt him."

And then he went off somewhere by himself, for he was soft-hearted, although a coward; he was planning to himself that when all the rest were asleep he would go to the pit, and pull his young brother up, and start him off on the road home, before any of them were stirring.

By this time Joseph was nearly at the tents. You can guess how his heart died in him when he saw the look on the faces of the nine big brothers waiting for him. They took him, and they tore the bright coat off him, and dragged him over the grass away to that

pit, and dropped him into it. There used to be water in it in the
time of the rains, but now in the summer it was dry. And there
they left him, and went back to their dinner. And Joseph sat on
the sand at the bottom of the pit, and looked up at the ring of blue
sky away at the top, and wondered how long it would be before
he died.

They were just in the middle of dinner when one of them happened to raise his head, and there—they had never heard it
coming, for the camels make no noise on the sand—there was a
caravan coming down the road, camels and camels and camels
padding along, with great loads swagging on either side of their
humps, spices and balm and sweet smelling things, and men driv-
ing them, dark-skinned men with fierce black eyes and long sharp
knives in their belts, and great white turbans. They were going on
down through Palestine, and away across the Desert, and so into
Egypt, and there they would sell the spices and the balm: the very
scents that the princess in Pharaoh's palace would sprinkle about
her room and pour into her bath. The brothers stood and watched
them swinging past, and suddenly Judah spoke out.

"What good will come of it if we leave Joseph to perish? We
will be guilty of his death and he is our brother. Let's sell him
instead to these foreign merchants."

It wasn't much kinder than the killing, for often the little slave
boys had a bad time; but there was a chance that he might get a
kind master who would keep him to wait on him at table and fan
him when he went to sleep. And I think after all Judah meant
well. So in a minute or two Joseph heard steps and voices coming
to the top of the pit, and a face looked down at him, and someone
let down a rope and told him to hold tight, and they hauled him
up into the sunlight again. At first he was glad, but they hurried
him over the grass to where the big dark-skinned men stood, and
he heard them wrangling about the price of something, and suddenly it flashed on him that the thing they were selling was himself. He turned to his brothers and he clung to them; long years
after they remembered how he had clung to them and how terribly
he cried, but it was too late then. Now they laughed at him; the
price was settled for twenty pieces of silver and Joseph was tied
and flung on one of the camels on top of the bales of spices, and

away the caravan swung on its way to the Desert, and the big brothers sat down to finish their dinner, and squabble over dividing the money.

Reuben came home about sunset and slipped quietly over to the pit and looked down. He could see nothing. He called, "Joseph! are you there?" and his own voice came back to him hollow. He had come too late. He rushed back to the tents wild with grief, and when they told him what they had done, he wasn't much better, for he was wondering how he would ever face his father. Then — it was a cruel thing to do — they took the gay little coat and dabbled it with blood from a kid that they had killed, and when they came back to the old black tent under the oak, and old Jacob came out to meet them, and asked where was Joseph, they showed him the little blood-stained coat. "We found this," they said, "look at it and see if it is your son's coat or not." The old man looked and knew it and cried out with a great cry, "It is my son's coat." It was Joseph's coat. He was dead. Joseph, his son, had been killed by a wild beast in the wilderness. For days Jacob mourned for him. It says that his sons tried to comfort him; I suppose they were sorry when they saw how terribly they had hurt him. But it was too late. The camels were hundreds of miles away, swinging across the Desert.

After many days the merchants and their camels had left the sand of the desert, and were going along through green fields, with palm trees by the road — grass so green that it reminded Joseph of the fields round Hebron in the spring. The man who drove his camel told Joseph that it was the land of Goshen, and the best land in Egypt; and "there," he said, pointing to a great cluster of palms and a gleam of white stone, "there is the City of the Sun."

They camped that night outside the city walls, but early in the morning they were astir, for they wanted a good place in the market-square. All the bales of sweet spices and frankincense and myrrh they piled up, and when the sun grew hot the whole square was fragrant with the perfumes that had come from Syria. There were plenty of buyers: all the drug-sellers in the City of the Sun were swarming like bees round the Midianites, wrangling and chaffing, and Joseph sat on an upturned cask and looked at the strange faces, and wondered if he would ever understand the strange words they used. Then a sudden silence fell, and he looked round, and the crowd had scattered, and the men who had brought him were on their faces uttering salutations, and there before him stood a splendid Captain of Pharaoh's Guard. He was passing through the square on his way home and smelt the perfumes. He stopped to buy white jars of spikenard for his wife and as he stood there his eyes fell on a fair-skinned boy among the black Midianite merchants, a handsome boy with great eyes staring at him, for never in his life had Joseph seen anything so magnificent as Potiphar, the Captain of Pharaoh's Guard.

The Captain smiled at him, for he saw the wonder in Joseph's eyes.

"And where do you come from?" he asked. He spoke in Egyptian and Joseph didn't understand and he shook his head, but he knew the voice was kindly, and he smiled back. Potiphar liked the quick way he had sprung to the ground when spoken to, and he liked the way the boy carried his head, and he liked the way he smiled. Then he turned to the sprawling Midianites and said, not quite so kindly, "Is the boy for sale?"

It was not five minutes before the bargain was struck and Joseph handed over. Potiphar had to pay dear for him, but he did not mind what he paid for a thing once he had set his heart on it. And off they swung, two soldiers of the Guard in front with drawn swords, then Potiphar alone, and Joseph a step or two behind him.

So Joseph became a slave in Egypt. He served his master well, and the Lord blessed all that he did. In time Potiphar gave Joseph charge of all his affairs, and whatever Joseph put his hand to prospered. One day after long hours supervising the work in the fields Joseph came from blazing heat into the great dim house, and down long corridors of cool marble, with the soft splash of water from the fountain in his ears. The house was very still, for all the slaves were at their work outside. He passed on steadily to his own room; for there were long accounts to be made up every day, and overseers were very exact in ancient Egypt. And then, above the splash of the fountain, he heard someone calling his name.

It was the voice of his mistress, Potiphar's wife, and he obeyed her and went, but, as he went, he was afraid. He had seen her first the evening Potiphar brought him home barefoot at his heels, and in the soft dusk of her room she had seemed to him like the first great star that comes into the sky after sunset. But even then she made him ill at ease, for there was something sinister about her, as if her beauty were the beauty of a snake. Always she was her most charming to him, but he feared her, for as he grew older, he saw that there was no honour in her. As much as he could he kept out of her way, but he could not avoid her altogether, because she was his master's wife, and Potiphar loved her.

She was beautiful but she had no shame. When Joseph came to her she told him that she cared for him—cared for him more than for the great Egyptian who was her husband. And then she prayed him to love her in return, and together they would deceive Potiphar. It was enough to turn Joseph's head to be told these things by a woman who had been set high above him like a star, but his answer is one of the finest things in the world. "Behold, my master hath given all that he hath into my hand, neither hath he kept anything back from me save thee, because thou art his wife. How then can I do this great wickedness and sin against God?" And with that he turned from her and went out.

Her anger was terrible. For she was beautiful, and proud of her beauty, and when she found that she could not make Joseph care for her she wanted only one thing and that was to punish him. And so when Potiphar came home that night he found her pacing up and down in her room in a frenzy, and she turned on him.

"See," she cried, "that Hebrew slave that you make so much of! He came into the house this day and insulted me—me, your wife. And when I cried out, he fled."

Potiphar would not believe her at first, but at last she goaded him into believing that Joseph was not what he had thought him—that he had been monstrously deceived. And a great gale of anger came on him, and he sent for Joseph, but Joseph would say nothing, for he would not speak against a woman. Then Potiphar clapped his hands, and two soldiers of the guard came in and took Joseph between them.

So Joseph went out from the presence of the Captain of the Guard, bound, between two soldiers. He was taken to the King's

Prison. And he lay that night, in the black dark of the dungeon, with chains on his hands and heavy fetters on his feet.

But after a short while the keeper of the prison looked kindly on him and took off the chains and fetters, and let him help with the duties in the prison, and as time went on he trusted Joseph more and more, till at last he gave the keys of the prison into his hand, and Joseph was left as much in charge as he had been in the old days with Potiphar. It was a change from being overseer of one of the greatest houses in Egypt to be warder in a dirty prison. But God blessed him in his work.

One day two men were brought in — two of the chief officers of Pharaoh's household, very fine and stately — the chief baker and the King's own cupbearer. Joseph was sorry for them, for he knew what it was like to be disgraced and put in prison after living in a great house, and he did his best to try and cheer them up. But one morning when he came in with their breakfasts, the two of them were sitting with their heads in their hands, looking so very wretched, that he set down the tray and asked what was the matter at all? And the cupbearer raised his head and said, "We had a wretched night; and we dreamt the queerest dreams. We don't know what they mean, but we're afraid something awful is going to happen." "Tell me them," said Joseph. "God is the only person who knows what dreams mean, and maybe He will show me." The chief baker shook his head, for he had a bad conscience, and he was sure his dream meant no good; but the cupbearer was an honest, jolly soul and he spoke out.

"I dreamt," he said, "that I saw a vine with three branches, and just while I was looking at it, green buds came on it, and then flowers, and before I knew there were big purple bunches of grapes. And it seemed to me Pharaoh's big gold drinking-cup was in my hand, and I squeezed the grapes into it with my fingers and gave it to the King just as I used to do." And Joseph said, "The three branches are three days. And it means that in three days Pharaoh will send for you, and forget that he ever was angry, and you'll be standing behind him, and pouring out his wine just like the old days." And then, suddenly, a great hope flashed into Joseph's mind. "And oh," he said, "when this happens and things are well with you, have me in your remembrance, and speak a word for me to Pharaoh, and bring me out of this house. Tell him that I was stolen away from my own country, and that I did nothing that they should put me in this dungeon." And then the baker plucked up heart and said to himself, "Maybe I haven't been found out after all," and told his dream—a stranger one still—about carrying three baskets on his head, with cakes and buns for Pharaoh on top, and how the birds came and pecked at them. Joseph shook his head very sadly. "It is not so well for you," he said. "Pharaoh has not forgotten. In three days you will be hanged."

True enough, the third day after that was Pharaoh's birthday, and even the prison hung out a flag. Towards evening there came a thundering knock at the door—"Open in the King's name"—and the King's messenger handed in two letters. The governor of the prison opened the first, and then turned to two of the soldiers, and they took the chief baker out and hanged him. Then he opened the second, and it was a Royal pardon, and a command that the cup-bearer should present himself at the Palace at once; for Pharaoh was giving a great dinner that night, and he wanted his old servant behind his chair. The cupbearer had been in a great state all day, and now Joseph begged that he might go and tell him the good news. And he stayed with him, and helped him to pack, and brushed him up, and off he went beaming, and vowing that he would speak to the King for Joseph that very night, and have him out in the morning.

Joseph thought to himself, "Who knows but this will be my last night in prison? Tomorrow I'll be out in the sun, and I'll go to the market and hire out as a camel-driver in a caravan, and to-morrow night I shall be in the desert sleeping under the stars, and after that it won't be long till I see the trees on the hill, and the old tent in Hebron again." He could not sleep for thinking of it, and he thought morning would never come. But it did come, morning, and noon, and afternoon, and evening, and brought no word. "It will come tomorrow," said Joseph, and he lay down and tried to sleep. But it did not come tomorrow, nor tomorrow, nor tomorrow, until Joseph gave up hoping, and went about his work with the heart in him dead. The cupbearer had forgotten.

A whole year went slowly round, and the King's birthday came again, and once again the flags went up, and a small hope stirred in Joseph's heart. "Surely," he said, "the cupbearer will remember where he was this time last year, and will speak for me to Pharaoh." But the cupbearer did not remember, and the night went by, and the year went by, and the great night came again. But this time there was no expectation in Joseph, only a great patience. He lay down and slept. And in the morning there came joy at last.

For that night Pharaoh slept ill, and when he did fall asleep it was to dream strange uneasy dreams. He dreamt that he was away from his palace, standing in deep grass beside the River Nile. And seven big cows came splashing up from the river, nice fat cows, and began grazing beside him. And then seven thin ugly cows, evil-looking beasts, came up after them, and gobbled up the fat cows, and in his consternation Pharaoh awoke, and wondered what had made him dream anything so ugly. Then he turned his pillow and fell asleep again. And no sooner was he asleep than he dreamed the same thing over again, but this time it was about seven yellow ears of corn, and seven ugly ones, black with the east wind, that ate them up. And once again he woke up and lay wide awake till morning. There was a great heaviness on him; he was certain that some great mischief was coming on himself or on his kingdom. And as soon as it was light, before even he had his breakfast, he sent for all the old wise men and magicians about the court, to ask them what was the meaning of his dreams. They stood before him in a row and stroked their shaven chins, and Pharaoh sat with his wine-cup untasted before him, and the fish cold on his plate, and stared at them with gloomy eyes. And one by one they said, "I give it up."

Suddenly the cupbearer gave a shout and clapped his hand to his head. "I do remember my faults this day," he said. "When my lord the King was angry with me and put me in prison there was a young man there, a Hebrew, and he was good to me. And one night, I dreamed a dream, and he read it for me, and it came true, and my lord the King sent for me that same day. And I have never thought about him from that day to this." "Bring him to me at once," Pharaoh said, and off went the cupbearer and the courtiers running.

And when Joseph had shaved and changed his clothes they brought him to Pharaoh.

Pharaoh said, "I dreamed a dream last night, and no one can read it. I have heard that you can read dreams."

"It is not in me," said Joseph. "God shall give Pharaoh an answer of peace."

Pharaoh said, "In my dream, behold, I stood upon the bank of the river: And, behold, there came up out of the river seven kine, fatfleshed and well favoured; and they fed in a meadow: And, behold, seven other kine came up after them, poor and very ill favoured and leanfleshed, such as I never saw in all the land of Egypt for badness: And the lean and the ill favoured kine did eat up the first seven fat kine: And when they had eaten them up, it could not be known that they had eaten them; but they were still ill favoured, as at the beginning. So I awoke. And I dreamed a second dream, and, behold, seven ears of corn came up in one stalk, full and good: And, behold, seven ears, withered, thin, and blasted with the east wind, sprung up after them: And the thin ears devoured the seven good ears: And I told this unto the magicians; but there was none that could declare it to me."

And Joseph listened. Then when Pharaoh had finished, he spoke. "The dreams are from God," he said. "He hath showed Pharaoh what He is going to do. The seven cows are seven years and the ears of corn are the same seven years, and the two dreams are one. The seven fat cows are seven years of plenty, and the seven lean cows are seven years of hunger, and it will be a great famine. Men will forget that they were ever anything but hungry, the hunger will be so great. So let Pharaoh do this. Let him look for a man, wise and discreet, and set him over all the land of Egypt. And let men be under him to gather in the fifth part of each harvest, and store it in the King's barns, against the days of hunger, that the people may not die."

Pharaoh turned to his councillors. "He has spoken wisely," he said, and they answered, "He has wisely spoken," for the terror of the hunger was upon them. "He has bidden me choose a wise man," said Pharaoh. "Is there any so wise as he with whom is the Spirit of God?" Then he turned to Joseph. "See," said Pharaoh,

"I have set thee over all the land of Egypt. Thou shalt be over my house, and over my people. I have given thee all things but my throne, only in that shall I be greater than thou." He took the ring from his own finger and put it on Joseph's, sent for the robes that only the nobles wore, and sent him out in his second chariot to make a progress through the streets, and the people fell on their knees as he went by. In the evening there was a great banquet. Joseph sat at Pharaoh's right hand, and they drank his health and acclaimed him. And Pharaoh gave him a new name, Zapnath-paaneah, and married him to a high-born Egyptian maiden, and made him ruler over all the land of Egypt.

The years passed as Joseph had foretold. The seven good years were over and done, and the famine had begun, and there were no crops in all the country-side, and the children cried for bread. And then the people began to see why the strange Governor had come round year after year and made them save some of their corn, and had stored it up in great barns in every town. It was there now for the buying, and the fathers went and bought it in sacks, and the mothers ground it and made bread and baked it. And after a while they began to see strange men coming along the roads, riding on camels and on donkeys, hungry-looking men who could speak no Egyptian but the word for corn. They were coming from all the countries outside Egypt, for there was bad harvesting and hunger everywhere, and Egypt was the only place where people had been wise enough to save. These strangers were going on to the City of the Sun, where the biggest barns were, for Joseph said that he would sell to the foreigners himself, and see to it that they were honest men and not spies. For there were spies in those days just as clever as they are now. Joseph was called the Governor of Egypt, and people talked about him as they talked about the King, and told stories about him, and how beautiful his wife was, and how fond he was of his little sons. For when the first boy was born Joseph was so utterly content that he called him Manasseh, which means Forgetfulness, for he said, "God has made me forget all my toil, and all my father's house."

One morning Joseph wakened early, early enough to hear the swallows talking to themselves in their nest under the eaves. And suddenly he seemed to remember the mornings years and years ago when he was little, and lay awake looking up at the black tent over his head, and heard the chirping of the birds in the old oak tree. And a strange hunger came on him to see it all again—the old black tent, and the smoke of the camp-fire, and his father sitting at the door. He remembered Benjamin, too, Benjamin just about the age of his own small son when Joseph bade him good-bye that morning. Of a sudden he felt lonely. It was all very well to be Governor of Egypt and the richest man under the King, to be great and stately and have people bowing down before you when you went through the streets. He wanted his own folk. He wanted somebody to call him "Joseph", not "my lord". His children called him father, and his wife called him by his great Egyptian name. There was not anybody to speak to him in his own tongue. He thought of the brothers who had sold him, and somehow all the anger at them had gone out of his heart. There was not one of them he would not have been glad to see.

All morning the old days kept coming back to him. He sat in the Chamber of Audience, and the slaves came and went, ushering in the foreigners who came with their gold to buy. But every now and then he dropped his head upon his hands and saw it all again—the tent door and the dogs asleep, and Benjamin digging with a pointed stick, and somewhere down the hill Reuben shouting at somebody to hurry up. He could have sworn that it was Reuben's voice, it was so near, and he raised his head, half thinking that his dream had come true. But he was in the Chamber of Audience, on his chair of state, with the lions on the steps, and at the far end of the hall the slaves had swung back the curtains and were ushering in a fresh crowd of buyers. Joseph looked at them wearily as they came slowly up the hall. There were ten of them, he counted, and they looked dusty and tired and travel-stained, as if they had come from afar. Their heads were bowed, for they were in the presence of the greatest man in Egypt, and his magnificence was a strange thing to them, and made them ill at ease. But as they fell on their faces before him, one of them shot a glance at the man they had come so far to seek, and Joseph met his eyes. It was only a moment, but it seemed to Joseph as if something had snapped in his heart. He rose to his feet and stood looking down at them where they lay before him. These were his brothers, and

they did not know him. And the man who held their life in his
hands was the boy they had sought to kill.

For a long time Joseph sat, holding the arms of his chair, and
gazing straight before him. There was silence in the place, for no
man may speak without leave in the presence of the King, and
Joseph was in the King's stead in Egypt. His brothers still knelt
bowed before him, and he sat high above them, looking and
remembering all things. Joseph roused himself.

"Whence come ye?" he said. He spoke in Egyptian and his
voice was harsh. His brothers sat back on their knees, and looked
at him fearfully. "My lord says 'Whence come ye?'" said the
interpreter. It was Judah who spoke. It was always Judah who
drove the bargains in the old days, Joseph remembered. Judah
was the business man of the family, far more than Reuben.

"From the land of Canaan we are come, to buy food," said
Judah. It was the first time Joseph had heard the old Hebrew
tongue for more than twenty years, and it went to his heart. But
he had his part to play, and he turned a blank face to the interpreter as if he had not known what had been said.

Then for a while he sat and frowned at them. "Ye be ten men,"
said Joseph. "Why are there ten of you journeying together? Ye
are spies—ye are come to see the weakness of the land."

"My lord," said Judah earnestly, "we are ten men journeying
together, because we are brothers, and we are come to buy food.
We are all sons of one father; we are true men, and not spies."

"Ye are spies," said Joseph, and his voice was level and hard.
"Ye are spies; to spy out the weakness of the land are ye come."

His brothers looked at one another in dread. "My lord," said
Judah desperately, "it is not so. Thy servants are brothers; there
are twelve of us altogether, and the youngest of us is this day
with our father and one—" he stopped. "But one," he said, "is
not."

Joseph rose to his feet. "Ye are spies," he said coolly. "If ye are
not, prove it. Let one of you go and bring your youngest brother,
that I may see if there is any truth in you, and the rest of you
shall be kept in prison till he comes. For I swear to you by the
life of Pharaoh"—the interpreter shook in his shoes—"ye shall not
go forth hence unless your youngest brother comes."

"Ho there!" he turned to the guard at the door. "Away with these to the King's Prison."

He sat in his chair and watched them marched out, and his face was the face of a graven image. "I will try them," he said to himself, "to see if there is any kindness in them, and if they have repented anything of their hardness of heart. But three days will be enough." In the morning of the third day he sent for them to his presence.

"Ye shall not die," he said, "if ye be true men. Let one of you be bound in the house of your prison, and let the rest of you go and carry corn for the hunger that is in your houses. But bring your youngest brother unto me. So shall I know that ye are true men, and ye shall live and not die."

They turned to one another, and to his surprise there was no relief in their faces. Joseph sat watching them with his hand over his eyes. They were talking despairingly, not knowing that he heard them. "It will kill the old man," they said, "if we take the boy from him. God forgive us! it is a judgment on us for what we did to our young stepbrother." Reuben had been sitting with his face in his hands, and now he looked up. "Did I not tell you?" he cried, "did I not tell you, 'Do not sin against the child?' and you would not hear. It is his blood that is required of us this day."

Joseph got up suddenly from his chair and went quickly out. Another minute and he would have broken down before them. But in a little while he set his face and came back to them, chose Simeon, and had him bound before their eyes. "Now go," he said, "and bring your youngest brother unto me, and I will deliver this brother unto you again." Only he told the steward to hide the money that they had paid for their corn in the mouth of every sack, and to give them things to eat on the road; and though they did not see him he stood behind the pillars of the doorway and watched them take the road, the road that he had so often travelled in his dreams, through the desert and over the hills to the green fields of home.

Once again Joseph sat in the Hall of Audience, and strangers came and went. It was months since the day that he saw his brothers coming up the hall, and sometimes he could have thought it was a dream; only that Simeon was still a hostage in the King's

Prison. "Will they ever come back, I wonder," he said to himself, "and will they bring Benjamin with them? Unless they are kinder than they used to be, my father will hardly trust them with him. It will go hard with the old man. I wonder was I right to make them bring him—if I shouldn't have told them at once who I was, and sent for them all to come. But if they are the same quarrelsome lot they used to be, they'd only be making mischief. I'll have to wait and see how they treat the boy."

There was a stir and commotion at the doorway, and the keeper of the door came in.

"Sir," he said, "here be the men from Syria, the brethren that ye took for spies."

"Is there a little lad with them?" said Joseph. "Nay," said the slave, "but a young man, well-grown and slender."

"Take them to my house," said Joseph, "and bid the steward make ready a feast, for they shall dine with me at noon."

It seemed a long morning to Joseph, watching the strangers come and go, but at last it wore to midday, and he was free.

"Did you make the men welcome?" he said to his steward, as he poured water over his hands. "They were sore afraid at first," said the steward, "for they thought you had meant to trap them for the money that was in their sacks, but I bade them be at ease, that God had given them the money, and I brought them water to wash their feet and fodder for the asses." "You have done well," said Joseph, and went into the hall.

They were prostrate on their faces as he came in. He saw the presents that their old father had sent him to soften his heart towards them, balm and honey and spices and myrrh and nuts and almonds. "Tell me," he said, "is your father well, the old man of whom ye told me? Is he yet alive?" They raised their heads and said, "Thy servant, our father, is yet alive." Joseph was looking them over one by one, and at last he saw a young face, not of the little Benjamin, digging in the sand, but not unlike the face that he used to see reflected in the fishponds when he went to measure the depth. "Is this the youngest brother?" he said softly. "God be gracious unto thee, my son," and with that he turned and went quickly out. Once in his own room he dropped his head in his hands and wept.

It was not for long. Joseph had learned to command himself in Egypt, and he dashed cold water on his face and went back, quiet and impassive. It was a wonderful feast, but more than all the strange dishes the brothers marvelled at Joseph himself. He had them placed at table as if he knew their ages—Reuben first, and Benjamin last, and he sent them dishes from his own table, though the best share always went to Benjamin. Joseph watched to see if it made them jealous, but they only seemed the better pleased. Joseph watched them laughing and teasing each other, the way brothers who like each other do, and his heart was very soft to them. Now and then they looked up at his table, with the great silver cup shining on it, and above it the Governor's grave, smiling face, and wondered how they had ever feared him.

They were to stay the night. Joseph sat late, but before he went to bed he sent for his steward.

"Let them be asleep," he said, "and then put their money in their sacks again, and in the sack of the youngest put my great silver cup; and rouse them for the road as soon as it is light." Joseph was waking early, and in the dawn he heard the clinking of hoofs in the yard, and the rattle of harness, and one of his brothers saying with a laugh, "Where's Benjamin? Is he never awake yet, the lazy little cub?" and Judah answering, "Let him have the last minute. I'll saddle for him." "Surely they are changed," thought Joseph, "but I must try them further yet." He lay waking for an hour, and then sent for his steward.

The brothers were beyond the city wall, and trotting along the east road, when they heard a horse galloping behind them. They halted and turned round. It was the steward of the Governor's house, and their hearts sank. He reined up before them and eyed them furiously. "Have ye no grace in you?" he said. "Was it not enough that my lord should feed you at his table, that ye must steal his own drinking cup? This is an evil thing that ye have done."

The brothers gazed at him in bewilderment. Then one spoke out. "God forbid that we should do this thing. Search us and see. And if you find the cup with any of us, he in whose sack it is found shall die, and we his brothers shall be my lord's slaves."

"Good," said the steward, "but we shall not be so hard with

you. He with whom it is found shall be the slave; the rest of you shall go your way blameless."

They got down from their asses, and one by one they opened their sacks. Beginning with the eldest, the steward passed from sack to sack till only Benjamin's was left. They opened it, and there gleaming in the corn lay the silver cup.

The steward turned and looked at them. Benjamin was staring at the cup with great bewildered eyes. The others were gazing at each other, dazed.

"I keep to my word," said the steward. "This youngster shall go back with us to answer for it, the rest of you go your ways."

The brothers rent their clothes. "We'll die first," they said. "Come, let us go together." Joseph, watching, saw the sorry little company clattering back into the yard, Judah—Judah who had sold him—riding beside Benjamin and comforting him.

"Thank God," he said, "I have seen their hearts at last." And so he rose and went down very stately to his judgment seat, and they came before their judge.

Joseph looked at them in silence. When he spoke, his voice was indifferent, almost mocking.

"What is this that ye have done?" he said. "Did ye think that I would not find you out?"

It was Judah who answered him, more bravely than he had ever spoken, and more desperately. He had come to the end of all things. "It is God who has found us out," he said, and he was thinking, not of this theft of the cup, but of that old sin against their brother. "Behold, we are thy slaves."

"God forbid," said Joseph. "He with whom the cup was found shall be my slave; the rest of you go in peace to your father."

Then Judah in his agony came a step nearer.

"Oh, my lord, let thy servant, I pray thee, speak a word in my lord's ears, and let not thine anger burn against thy servant; for thou art even as Pharaoh.

"My lord asked his servants, saying, 'Have ye a father, or a brother?' and we said unto my lord, 'We have a father, an old man, and a child of his old age, a little one; and his brother is dead, and he alone is left of his mother, and his father loveth him.' And thou saidst unto thy servants, 'Bring him down unto me that

I may set mine eyes upon him.' And we said unto my lord, 'The lad cannot leave his father; for if he should leave his father, his father would die.' And thou saidst unto thy servants, 'Except your youngest brother come down with you, ye shall see my face no more.'

"And it came to pass when we came up unto my father, we told him the words of my lord. And our father said, 'Go again and buy us a little food.' And we said, 'We cannot go down; if our youngest brother be with us, then will we go down: for we may not see the man's face, except our youngest brother be with us.' And my father said unto us, 'Ye know that my wife bare me two sons; and the one went out from me, and I said, "Surely he is torn in pieces"; and I saw him not since; and if ye take this also from me, and mischief befall him, ye shall bring down my grey hairs with sorrow to the grave.'

"Now, therefore, when I come to my father, and the lad be not with us; seeing that his life is bound up in the lad's life; it shall come to pass, when he seeth that the lad is not with us, that he will die: and thy servants shall bring down the grey hairs of our father, with sorrow to the grave. For thy servant became surety for the lad unto my father, saying, "If I bring him not unto thee, then I shall bear the blame to my father for ever."

"Now therefore, I pray thee, let thy servant abide instead of the lad, a bondman to my lord: and let the lad go up with his brethren. For how shall I go up to my father, and the lad be not with me? Lest peradventure I see the evil that shall come on my father."

Joseph turned to the Egyptians looking on. "Go out from me," he cried, and they went out wondering, and left him alone with his brethren. And Joseph bowed his head and wept aloud.

Then at last he spoke—"I am Joseph," he said. "Doth my father yet live?" His brothers stood and looked at him, and could not answer, for they were troubled and amazed. "Come near to me," said Joseph and held out his hands to them, and they came slowly near. "I am Joseph, your brother," he said, speaking very slowly, that they might take it in, "whom ye sold into Egypt. But you are not to be grieved or angry with yourselves, for God sent me before you to preserve life. For these two years hath the famine been in the land: and there are still five years to come, in which there shall be neither ploughing nor harvest. And God sent me before you to save your lives by a great deliverance. And He has made me a father to Pharaoh, and lord of his house, and ruler of all Egypt. And now, make haste and go to my father and say to him, 'Thy son, Joseph, says: God hath made me lord of all Egypt; come down unto me, and thou shalt dwell in the land of Goshen, and shalt live near me, thou and thy children and grandchildren, and all thy flocks and thy herds, and I will feed thee.'

"You see with your own eyes, and my brother Benjamin sees, that it is I who speak to you. And tell my father of all my glory in Egypt, and of all that ye have seen; and ye must haste and bring my father here."

And then he turned and held out his arms to Benjamin and embraced him. And one by one his brothers came up and he kissed them every one, and after that, it says, they all talked with him.

And so the story goes back to where it began, with an old man sitting at the door of the big black tent, in Hebron, and watching for his sons; and it tells how they came with a great caravan, and how they told the wonderful news, and the old man's heart fainted. He could not believe them. Again and again they told him what Joseph had said, but still he shook his head, and then Judah took his arm and said, "Come and see the fine carriage he sent to bring you to him." And when Jacob saw the carriage and the wagons that Joseph had sent to bring him into Egypt, then his spirit revived. "It is enough," he said, "Joseph my son, is yet alive; I will go and see him before I die."

OISIN'S MOTHER

It happened one time when Finn and his men were coming back from the hunting, that a beautiful fawn started up before them, and they followed it, men and dogs, till at last they were all tired

and fell back, all but Finn himself and his hounds, Bran and Sceolan. And suddenly as they were going through a valley, the fawn stopped and lay down on the smooth grass, and Bran and Sceolan came up with it, and they did not harm it at all, but went playing about it, licking its neck and its face.

There was wonder on Finn when he saw that, and he went on home to Almhuin, and the fawn followed after him playing with the hounds, and it came with them into the house at Almhuin. And when Finn was alone late that evening, a beautiful young woman having a rich dress came before him, and she told him it was she herself was the fawn he was after hunting that day. "And it is for refusing the love of Doirche, the Dark Druid of the Men of Dea," she said, "that I was put in this shape. And through the length of three years," she said, "I have lived the life of a wild deer in a far part of Ireland, and I am hunted like a wild deer. And a serving-man of the Dark Druid took pity on me," she said, "and he said that if I was once within the dun of the Fianna of Ireland, the Druid would have no more power over me. So I made away, and I never stopped through the whole length of a day till I came into the district of Almhuin. And I never stopped then till there was no one after me but only Bran and Sceolan, that have human wits; and I was safe with them, for they knew my nature to be like their own."

Then Finn gave Sadbh his love, and took her as his wife, and she stopped in Almhuin. And so great was his love for her, he gave up his hunting and all the things he used to take pleasure in, and gave his mind to no other thing but herself.

But at last the men of Lochlann came against Ireland, and their ships were in the bay below Beinn Edair, and they landed there.

And Finn and the battalions of the Fianna went out against them, and drove them back. And at the end of seven days Finn came back home, and he went quickly over the plain of Almhuin, thinking to see Sadbh his wife looking out from the dun, but there was no sign of her. And when he came to the dun, all his people came out to meet him, but they had a very downcast look. "Where is the flower of Almhuin, beautiful gentle Sabdh?" he asked them. And it is what they said: "While you were away fighting, your

likeness, and the likeness of Bran and of Sceolan appeared before
the dun, and we thought we heard the sweet call of the horn of
the Fianna. And Sabdh, that was so good and so beautiful, came
out of the house," they said, "and she went out of the gates, and
she would not listen to us, and we could not stop her. 'Let me go
meet my love,' she said, 'my husband, the father of the child that
is not born.'

"And with that she went running out towards the shadow of
yourself that was before her, and that had its arms stretched out
to her. But no sooner did she touch it than she gave a great cry,
and the shadow lifted up a hazel rod, and on the moment it was
a fawn standing on the grass. Three times she turned and made
for the gate of the dun, but the two hounds the shadow had with
him went after her and took her by the throat and dragged her
back to him. And by your hand of valour, Finn," they said, "we
ourselves made no delay till we went out on the plain after her.
But it is our grief, they had all vanished, and there was not to be
seen woman, or fawn or Druid, but we could hear the quick tread
of feet on the hard plain, and the howling of dogs. And if you
would ask every one of us in what quarter he heard those sounds,
he would tell you a different one."

When Finn heard that, he said no word at all, but he struck
his breast over and over again with his shut hands. And he went
then to his own inside room, and his people saw him no more
for that day, or till the sun rose over Magh Life on the morrow.

And through the length of seven years from that time, whenever
he was not out fighting against the enemies of Ireland, he went
searching and ever searching in every far corner for beautiful
Sadbh. And there was great trouble on him all the time, unless
he might throw it off for a while hunting or in battle. And through
all that time he never brought out to any hunting but the five
hounds he had most trust in, Bran and Sceolan and Lomaire and
Brod and Lomluath, for that way there would be no danger for
Sadbh if ever he came on her track.

But after the end of seven years, Finn and some of his chief men
were hunting on the sides of Beinn Gulbain, and they heard a
great outcry among the hounds, that were gone into some narrow

place. And when they followed them there, they saw the five
hounds of Finn in a ring, and they keeping back the other hounds,
and in the middle of the ring was a young boy, with high looks,
and he naked and having long hair. And he was no way daunted
by the noise of the hounds, and did not look at them at all, but
at the men that were coming up. And as soon as the fight was
stopped Bran and Sceolan went up to the little lad, and whined
and licked him that any one would think they had forgotten their
master. Finn and the others came up to him then, and put their
hands on his head, and made much of him. And they brought him
to their own hunting cabin, and he ate and drank with them, and
before long he lost his wildness and was the same as themselves.
And as to Bran and Sceolan, they were never tired playing about
him.

And it is what Finn thought, there was some look of Sadbh in
his face, and that it might be he was her son, and he kept him
always beside him. And little by little when the boy had learned
their talk, he told them all he could remember. He used to be
with a deer he loved very much, he said, and that cared and
sheltered him, and it was in a wide place they used to be, having
hills and valleys and streams and woods in it, but that was shut
in with high cliffs on every side, that there was no way of escape
from it. And he used to be eating fruits and roots in the summer,
and in the winter there was food left for him in the shelter of a
cave. And a dark-looking man used to be coming to the place,
and sometimes he would speak to the deer softly and gently, and
sometimes with a loud angry voice. But whatever way he spoke,
she would always draw away from him with the appearance of
great dread on her, and the man would go away in great anger.
And the last time he saw the deer, his mother, the dark man was
speaking to her for a long time, from softness to anger. And at the
end he struck her with a hazel rod, and with that she was forced
to follow him, and she looking back all the while at the child, and
crying after him that any one would pity her. And he tried hard
to follow after her, and made every attempt, and cried out with
grief and rage, but he had no power to move, and when he could
hear his mother no more he fell on the grass and his wits went
from him. And when he awoke it is on the side of the hill he was,

where the hounds found him. And he searched a long time for the place where he was brought up, but he could not find it.

And the name the Fianna gave the lad was Oisin, and it is he was their maker of poems, and their good fighter afterwards.

SOME NOTES ON SOURCES

Acknowledgements for permission to use copyright material appear elsewhere, but storytellers and those working with books for children may like more details and information about the stories in this book.

THE APPLE OF CONTENTMENT. An original fairy tale by Howard Pyle, the American writer and illustrator, from *Pepper and Salt* (Harper, 1895), one of his earliest books. All I have done to this story is to alter the archaic style of conversation.

CAPORUSHES, from *English Fairy Tales* retold by Flora Annie Steel (Macmillan, 1927).

THE FEATHER OF FINIST THE FALCON from Post Wheeler's *Russian Wonder Tales* (1921) reissued in 1947 by A. S. Barnes and Co. Inc.

HOW IAN DIREACH GOT THE BLUE FALCON, slightly adapted from Lang (*Orange Fairy Book*, 1898), who gives the source as *Tales of the West Highlands*.

THE LAD WHO WENT TO THE NORTH WIND, from Asbjornsen; Sir George Webbe Dasent's translation in *Popular Tales from the Norse* (1859).

LITTLE FOOL IVAN AND THE LITTLE HUMPBACK HORSE. A favourite story with children, who find the quaint little horse very appealing. This story, which has incidents in common with other Russian fairy tales and at least one close parallel in "The Horse of Power", may have its origin in the considerably longer story in verse by Yershov, two translations of which (to my knowledge) have appeared in English. Not finding an entirely satisfactory text I have adapted and retold from different versions.

ALI BABA AND THE FORTY THIEVES. A long story which I think Laurence Housman handled expertly in a book published by Hodder and Stoughton for Boots with illustrations by Dulac.

Some Notes on Sources

BEOWULF AND GRENDEL. I am grateful to Rosemary Sutcliff for approving an extract assembled from Chapters 2, 3 and 4 from her *Beowulf* (Bodley Head, 1961).

THE BIRTH OF PRYDERI is from *Welsh Legends and Folk Tales* (Oxford, 1955) retold by Gwyn Jones. Thomas Jones and Gwyn Jones have translated the *Mabinogion* (Dent, Everyman, 1949).

FINN AND THE YOUNG HERO'S CHILDREN. A crisp and evocative telling of this story from the Finn cycle (from Argyllshire) included by Norah and William Montgomerie in their book of Scottish folk tales *The Well at the World's End* (Hogarth Press, 1956).

GARETH AND LINETTE is by Barbara Leonie Picard, from her *Stories of King Arthur and His Knights* (Oxford, 1955); these are twelve separate stories. *King Arthur and his Knights of the Round Table* by Roger Lancelyn Green (Faber, 1957) is a continuous history of Arthur's kingdom. *Legends of King Arthur and his Knights* by Sir J. Knowles (Warne, n.e. 1958) is a nineteenth-century version of Malory, read by Tennyson when he was working on *The Idylls of the King*. *King Arthur and the Round Table* is retold by A. M. Hadfield (Dent, 1953) in continuous narrative from the standpoint of the Quest of the Holy Grail.

HOW CORMAC MAC ART GOT HIS BRANCH is retold by F. M. Pilkington in *Shamrock and Spear* (Bodley Head, 1966). F. M. Pilkington has also movingly retold *The Three Sorrowful Tales of Erin* ("The Fate of the Children of Tuireann", "The Fate of the Children of Lir" and "Deirdre and the Sons of Uisne". Bodley Head, 1965).

JOSEPH AND HIS BRETHREN is condensed from *Stories of Holy Writ* by Helen Waddell (Constable, 1949). *Stories from the Bible* by Walter de la Mare (Faber, 1929; n.e. 1977) includes the lives of Moses, Samson, Saul and David.

OISIN'S MOTHER is from Lady Gregory's *Gods and Fighting Men* (Murray, 1904). The story of Cuchulain has been retold by Rosemary Sutcliff — *The Hound of Ulster* (Bodley Head, 1963).